I0567293

<u>Flipping Fate</u>
By Judy Dawn

Books By Judy Dawn
The Men of Snow series
Dragon Ring Legend Series

Flipping Fate

A PubIndie Book
Published by Judy Dawn
Seattle, WA
www.judydawn.com

First Edition: Dec. 2014
Printed by Create Space

Chapter 1

Charlie Davies held tight to her oversized umbrella after stepping off the bus. Snuggled in her jacket, she hustled toward the nearby tea shop. The streetlamps flickered on for the night and she calmed the anxiety in her belly with a long inhale.

A cold evening breeze pinched the skin on her exposed nose and cheeks. Tonight's miserable weather continued a three-day rainstorm over western Washington. She stomped her rain-booted feet through shallow puddles on the soaked sidewalk.

A deep hole in the cement stopped her short of the shop. Stepping around it, she saw a golden flash. *What could it be?* she thought, squinting through the murky street water.

Charlie squatted next to the hole.

As she reached into the pool of water, her fingers stung from the cold. She hissed and jerked her hand out and shook the water from her fingers. Her fist trembled as she blew a warm breath into her cupped hand.

She took a breath, looked away. Muted voices bounced around the strip mall. Most of the stores were closed and dark. A washed-out sunset threw pale light onto a row of parked cars in front of the busy Green Leaf and Brew shop. Strangers hurried in and out of the one-story building.

She glanced at the hole again.

The gold sparkled, teased, tempted.

She shot her hand into the water a second time and ground her teeth against the freezing water. Her impulsive actions stirred the dirt in the puddle. She lost sight of the golden item.

If she couldn't see it, she couldn't grab it.

Her fingertips numbed, palm burned, and her wrist ached. Frowning, she eased her hand from the water.

A warm item floated into Charlie's palm. She smiled and clung to the prize. Then she studied it. It was a coin, but not a machine-made coin. It seemed handcrafted and old. Heavy. The edges were smooth but made an awkward, asymmetrical circle. She spotted shiny flecks imbedded in the metal.

When she rubbed the dirt off with her thumb, two Fs appeared back to back. The relief was crudely designed. On the other side, more words were carved, not as charming as the front letters. These words read: FLIP YOUR FATE.

Thunder roared and the rain thickened, cascading over the edge of her umbrella.

Charlie glanced up. Nobody else was in the rain. A strong gust of wind sent an uneasy tremble down her spine. She stood, tucked the coin into her purse, and hurried around the pothole toward the Green Leaf and Brew.

Warmth washed over her when she stepped inside. Her numb fingers tingled and she sighed as she shook the rain from her umbrella and set it in the box beside the door.

Her eyes took a moment adjusting to a thick cloud of bittersweet smoke. She wasn't the tallest in the room. On her toes, she searched for Lance Dixon's face within the crowd.

The friendly intern had helped her pack her office on Monday after she quit. During the move, Lance noticed her extensive tea assortment. He had confessed that he worked at the Green Leaf and Brew, earning extra cash as a night barista. He suggested that she stop by the store some night for a tour.

She initially told him that she wasn't interested, but sitting alone in her apartment for three days had changed her mind.

Charlie covered a light cough and made her way to a loaded bookshelf on the left side of the shop. Laughing and talking voices replaced the pitter-patter of raindrops on the front windows. She smiled at the new energy surrounding her in an upbeat flow.

Over the wooden shelving she studied the eccentric crowd. Some wore dreadlocks. Others had mismatched, dated clothes. Flannel over-shirts seemed the popular choice.

The last time she had attended a busy Friday night party, on Clyde Hill near Seattle, nobody seemed this genuinely happy. Maybe her decision to move into a different area was right.

She covered her designer shirt by closing her damp jacket, and then perused the titles on the bookshelf. She didn't recognize any of them. A handwritten sign atop the shelves said the books were by local authors.

That explained her confusion. She read bestsellers. With mass-market sales, she was guaranteed an entertaining read for the expense. There was a book titled *Money Is Happiness.*

She stroked the upper edge of a handmade book and frowned.

"That's a good book."

She jumped at a male voice.

Its owner stood a head taller than her. His turtleneck-covered torso was wider than any she had ever seen. He had short, smoke-black hair slicked away from his thick eyebrows and a compelling stare.

He casually shoved his hands in his front pockets, unthreatening. "I've read that one myself and recommend it. Besides, you can't go wrong with three bucks for a night of entertainment, right?"

His sinfully long lashes framed extraordinary nutmeg-colored eyes, flecked and ringed with gold. Naturally tanned skin covered his bold, clean-shaven jaw line. Charlie considered his full lips, and he glanced to her right and his smile straightened.

"Charlie?" Lance's familiar voice lured her attention. The smaller man drew her into his arms for an awkward hug. The sleeves of his fitted Arrow shirt were rolled up to his elbows. "I'm surprised to see you here."

She uncomfortably patted his back and stepped away. "Hi, Lance. I thought I'd come and see the original tea selection you told me about."

"Well, you chose a great night to come by. We have a local group about to get up on the stage." He looked at the man beside her. "I see you've met my new assistant, Mr. Green."

"Zander." He held out a beefy palm.

Not the hands of an office worker. Charlie found his rough palms fascinating. The golden Rolex that peeked out from under his cheap sweater sleeve was even more interesting. A J.C. Penney shirt with a genuine Rolex watch.

"Nice watch."

He yanked his hand back and slid his sleeve over the watch. His eyes narrowed at her. "Have I seen you somewhere before?"

She doubted he subscribed to Mercer Island's exclusive magazine: *People in Business*. She offered a polite smile. "I, ah, don't think so."

"Come on." Lance cut in. He glared at Zander. "The guy is nothing but trouble."

Zander's grin slanted and he winked.

"Come on." Lance dragged Charlie's shoulder, guiding her away from Zander. "I'll help you find a good seat for the performance, then after, I'll spend more time showing you the tea. I can hang your jacket if you want."

"No, that's okay. Thanks anyway." She adjusted her purse onto her shoulder. She allowed Lance to lead her with a hand at her lower back. "Why is Zander trouble?"

"He's a good guy. Just complicated." He paused and looked at her. "Sorry I can't chat more right now. I've got to get back to the counter. The guys are fast at filling drink orders, but it can turn into a madhouse right before performance time."

Charlie knew that joint cover night in downtown Seattle's Pioneer Square, with Cowgirls and Doc Maynard's central to the First and Second Avenue bar scene, could turn into a madhouse on Friday nights. But this place was located in Redmond, outside of Bellevue. And Bellevue was comparatively sedate suburbia, east of Seattle, and in Charlie's opinion couldn't be that big of a problem when it came to crowds.

They rushed by a jewelry counter, passed a set of smaller tables, and ended up in a square lounge at the back of the shop. He said, "Take the chair beside the couch. Best seat in the house."

"Okay, thanks." Charlie smiled.

Lance hurried behind the bar. Charlie adjusted her Gucci bag beside her and looked around. A beat-up, dark wood table separated her and a couple lounging on a loveseat, sharing a cup of something.

They glanced at her, undoubtedly wondered what she was doing here in her hundred-dollar rain boots, tailored black slacks, and Eddie Bauer puff jacket. She felt like a Wall Street broker managing million-dollar accounts, dropped into a group of penny stock co-investors.

But Charlie liked the way she looked. She liked her unruly, dark hair in a tamed bun at the back of her neck. She also had the smoothest skin from the best products on the market. If they did their job, then she appeared younger than her twenty-four years. Growing up with money had its privileges and its downfalls.

The woman on the loveseat looked at her again. She wore a beanie and had a huge black earring in one ear, making an empty ring-hole. The piercing in her lip sparkled.

"Crazy weather tonight, isn't it?" Charlie tried. Usually June weather was hot and dry. Today was warm but sticky with high humidity.

The woman didn't respond and started another private conversation with her stringy-haired friend. The "private" part was accentuated by the woman's turned back.

If Beth were here for coaching, Charlie's socializing efforts would go easier. Her best friend knew all the right things to say and do at parties. Charlie knew numbers.

Anxiety tightened the muscles in Charlie's neck as she studied the muted green-striped wallpaper on the ceiling.

Her phone rang from an outside pocket in her bag. Without looking at the caller identification, she answered. "Hello?"

"You quit while I was out of town?" said her ex-husband and boss, Kenneth Oliver. "And you've been gone for a week without someone to manage the place?"

Kenneth had left town for The Montreal Fireworks Festival. It was a major annual international competition, the best and largest fireworks festival in the world. Pyrotechnical companies from different countries presented a thirty-minute-long pyromusical show. The exposure from the competition's biweekly shows increased business revenues every year for Western Flashworks—the company Charlie quit earlier that week.

"Did you win the competition?"

"Did I win?" Kenneth's angry tone plunged her into a hole of darkness. "Would I be back here, talking with you, like this, if I had won?"

No. He would be on the road doing interviews with high-paying clients.

Her heart raced, heat crawled through her body, and she shrunk deeper into the chair. "I left my number if someone had any questions," Charlie said. "There's nothing big going on. The ledgers are up to date till the end of the month. That's plenty of time to find a new replacement."

"That makes it all better?"

Apparently not. Her gut twisted. The short notice was not her style. She wasn't naturally impulsive.

"I have been killing myself for the last month, putting together show after show to get this company off the ground. I'm thinking everything is going fine back home because the CFO, my wife, is on duty. Instead, I find out you leave on Monday without a replacement."

She covered the heat in her cheeks with a shaking hand like the bill of a baseball cap on her forehead. "Yes, um, I—"

"Nobody has been bookkeeping for a week!" He exhaled through the line. "Look. I'll let you make this right. I'll tell everyone the notice that you quit was an ... emotional outburst."

Her mouth fell open. "What?"

He spoke fast. "Thank goodness you locked your office when you left. Nobody knows you took your stuff out. I expect to see you back at your desk on Monday morning—like always. Am I clear?"

"You're very clear, but—"

"Good." The line went dead.

She stared at the phone between her shaking fingers. Why did she freeze up when Kenneth spoke to her? Why couldn't she tell him to back off? Other people, normal people, told him all the time. He didn't like it, but he adjusted his behavior for them. Kenneth's short temper and overloaded ego were the second and third reasons she had divorced him. His failure to listen was the fourth reason.

Emotional outburst? She didn't believe anyone at Flashworks would believe that lie. She had kept her emotions out of the workplace. Despite her urges. Did it matter anymore? Not really. She didn't intend to go back.

Grinding noises from the coffee and tea bar drew her attention. She studied the three men behind the counter, laughing and smiling while they worked. They hustled as if they were square dancing in the confined space.

The small crowd grew rowdier with each minute. Eager energy vibrated in the air, and goosebumps rose along her covered forearms. The heat grew inside her body and she unzipped her jacket.

Across the room, in front of her, a spotlight marked the stage. A young blonde woman stepped onto the stage with a guitar and applause broke out.

In high school, Charlie had loved choir.

The composed performer smiled and thanked the crowd for a warm welcome. She stroked the strings on her guitar, and a throaty yowl vibrated through the speakers. The sheet behind her lifted and revealed her band.

The energy in the room thundered.

The blonde laughed, looked back at the band, and bobbed her head. Chest-pounding bass accompanied earsplitting wails from her guitar. The lead singer's haunted tone married with the mix.

People started jumping, fists pumping the air. Men slammed their upper bodies into another's matching the beats in the music.

The couple on the couch stood and groped each other. Maybe they were dancing. Charlie couldn't really tell. She eased out of her chair and headed for the door. Her shoulders hunched forward, protecting her assets from wandering hands, as bodies invaded her personal space. Dizzy, she lifted a shielding forearm against a set of guys ramming into each other.

Then strong fingers clamped around her bicep and yanked her off-balance.

Her body crashed into a giant man. Sweat dripped from his forehead onto his t-shirt-covered shoulders. The pungent odor of ammonia assaulted her senses. Her mouth dried and the smoke thickened around them. She couldn't catch her breath.

She wiggled like a little fish on an obsessed fisherman's hook. The man's strength overwhelmed her. He rubbed his body against hers. Some sort of dance, maybe.

Lance appeared next to her with Zander, who pulled her away, hugged her against him, and guided her toward the door. His big torso protected her from overzealous bodies.

They hurried through the door and cool air brushed her heated skin. Zander's hands gently held her biceps. "Breathe."

Charlie did.

"Good. Again." The gold flecks in his eyes shimmered with his concern.

She focused, inhaled, and the anxiety lifted. The enclosing walls were gone. In their place was his quiet confidence and compelling stare. She exhaled. Her heartbeat slowed. "Who was that guy?"

Zander shrugged. "Lance knows him."

Charlie shook her head, blinked, and then rubbed her temples. "I don't know what happened. I guess I just ... I was so confused."

"That's more than cigarette smoke in there." His calm voice helped her establish a balance. "I take it you don't smoke."

She shook her head and gestured for him to let her go. "I'm okay now." She shook her arms freely. "I'm just sad I didn't get a chance to see the tea collection."

"Lance wanted me to give you this." He retrieved a small package from his back pocket and handed it to her. "He said he'd call you later."

"Oh, thanks." She tucked the package into her bag. The light on her phone in her purse exposed the time. "I've got to head home now."

"I'll walk you to your car."

"I didn't drive."

"Oh." He shoved his hands in the front pockets of his jeans. "How are you getting home?"

"The bus." She should leave. Instead, she hesitated. The moment turned awkward. Her heart raced. "I'm, ah, I'm late. I've got to hurry to catch the last one. Thanks for the, ah, rescue."

"Sure. Yeah." The words fell fast out of his mouth. A moonbeam highlighted half of his hard-edged features, sculpted cheekbones and kinked nose.

He was not her typical type. She usually went for the slim, awkward, and funny nerds. Zander's eyes were dreamy and his athletic body—

"I'm not comfortable letting you walk to the stop on your own. Mind if I walk with you to make sure you get on safely?"

Her mood lifted. "If it's not to much trouble."

"It's not." He turned with her and started walking. "I swear I've seen you before. Are you a model or something?"

She laughed. "Thanks for the compliment, but I'm just an out-of-work accountant."

He nodded. "How did you meet Lance?"

She explained, and her thoughts drifted back to her former job. Her recall of Kenneth's orders to return on Monday ratcheted the muscles in her shoulders. She tightened her jacket around the front of her body against a sudden chill.

"Have you met his sister?"

She looked at Zander's strong profile. "Lance has a sister?"

"A wife too." He studied his steps. Something in his tone stopped her short of the bus stop. He looked at her then. Even under the dim streetlight, she noted the innuendo in his stare. His eyebrows rose. "Just wondering if you knew."

Her mild interest in Zander plummeted. "Yes. I know."

The city bus huffed to a stop on the corner a few feet from their position.

If Zander could think she would have an affair with a married man, he was a jerk. She brushed past him and climbed on board without looking back. "Bye."

"Hey, wait. I—aw, shit."

The bus doors closed between them. Nobody else was on the bus and she found a seat near the front. Thank goodness she hadn't missed the last run of the night because of him. She figured she would stick with the nerds. They thought about more than sex.

After she caught the joint bus from Redmond to Bellevue, she fished her phone from her pocket and speed-dialed Bethany Hardgrave, her best friend since freshman year at Stanford. Charlie could tell her anything.

Well, almost anything.

"Hey Charlie. Did you still go out even though I wasn't there?"

"Yes." Charlie glanced out the window at nothing. "Sort of. I mean. I met some new people tonight. I tried talking with them, but it didn't go so well. I wish I were better at it. Like you."

"Meeting new people gets easier. You'll get the hang of it and you won't need me there. You've got to keep trying."

"I will. That's why I moved out of the mansion. Everyone I knew there was part of my father's business. I couldn't tell if they liked me or were just trying to get closer to him."

"I understand." Bethany paused. "Where are you now?"

"I'm on the bus headed home."

"Well, I'm looking forward to seeing you tomorrow."

Charlie untwisted the purse strap on her shoulder. "It'll be great to see you too."

"I'm sorry I couldn't help you move the rest of your stuff earlier this week. My brother…"

"Don't worry about it." Charlie realized the bus had passed her corner. Her hands shook as she yanked the cord for the next stop. "Got to go, see you soon."

"Okay. Bye." Bethany disconnected.

Streetlights lined the sidewalk. Charlie stepped off the bus and paused, cautious. She wasn't far from her apartment building. The streets of downtown Bellevue weren't crowded. A few homeless people were hunkered down in the shadows, but she could walk home safely.

She lifted her chin to the evening sky and marched toward her new apartment. Her mind wandered back to Zander's questions.

Infidelity was the first reason she divorced Kenneth.

Kenneth got most of their acquired belongings in their divorce settlement, which had become final on Monday, which was what drove her to suddenly quit. They didn't have much in the bank to split anyway. It turned out he had kept a side account for himself, in his name, and she didn't have any legal right to it. He was better off than she was at the moment.

Guilt hit her chest with the thud of her heartbeat. She was a good accountant. She should have discovered his second account.

Absentmindedly, she reached into her purse for the coin she discovered earlier. Light reflected on the tiny golden speckles in the metal. She rubbed her thumb over the etched words: FLIP YOUR FATE.

Her toe caught on the sidewalk. Her knee hit the hard ground and the purse flew off her arm. The coin flipped out of her hand, bouncing onto the concrete with an echoing ting. Her palms slapped the cold sidewalk and then her chin cracked against the surface. Her teeth bit into her tongue and she closed her eyes.

After a moment, she released a held breath and swore.

When the pain ebbed, she spit a mouthful of blood past the curb and looked behind her. An uneven sidewalk crack jutted up, like a miniature Cascade Mountain range. She shook her head.

At the corner of her apartment building, a small shadow snaked toward her fallen position. She studied the shadow while she reached for her purse.

Pins and needles jabbed along her arms. She moved her tongue over her teeth, winced, and then push-upped from the damp ground to a sitting position. She inhaled.

Meow, the emerging shadow said.

She leveled into a squat and then held out a hand. "Hey, kitty?"

The kitten rubbed his cheek against her outstretched, trembling fingers. Something inside her warmed.

"Aren't you cute."

He purred against her palm.

She noticed the coin under the kitten's black paw. Her steady fingers picked it up. A flash of gold drew her attention to the writing. Moments before, it had said: FLIP YOUR FATE.

Now the etching read: ADOPT THE STRAY. A set of numbers, 1/21, curved along the bottom edge of the coin face.

She looked from the coin to the kitten and back. "What in the world?"

The coin heated in her palm. Questions exploded in her head. Was it magic? How could that be? She didn't believe in magic. Yet, somehow, the words on the coin changed. She didn't imagine it. She turned the coin in her palm. Each F, in crude, raised letters, hadn't changed.

The kitten shifted closer to her and brushed against her sore knee.

"But my apartment building doesn't approve of pets." She stared at the tiny animal, so cute and vulnerable. She couldn't leave it out here all night. Alone. He was lost in this big city without help.

She glanced around at the empty street, and then back at the kitten. "Okay, friendly shadow, it's a risk. You're going to have to ride quietly inside my purse if you want a warm place to sleep tonight." She scooped up the little ball of fur and groaned when she stood. It didn't take long to secure the stray into her bag.

He was small, thin, and willing.

Charlie secured the coin in a pocket of her purse and approached the entrance gates of her building. The gates stayed open during the day for deliveries and visitors. She typed in her security code and the iron gates clacked open. She shoved through, wanting a warm bath and some sleep.

A fairly clean, uncovered, six-foot porch led to the front door. Nest Apartment's call buttons lined on the right wall. At the door, she typed her code into another keypad and the door squeaked open on its hinges.

Meow.

"Shush, we talked about this, remember?" she whispered to the stowaway and shut the door behind them.

Her landlord, Milton Green, lived on the first level. His apartment door sat on the far side of a mudroom. A soft overhead light didn't reach the corners of the entry space. Storage for the tenants was through a door on the right and on the left was the stairs.

She hurried up the oak staircase, but Mr. Green's door flew open before she got far. Extra light from his apartment, music and shouting, jarred her nerves. The kitten wasn't a smart move. If she got caught with a pet—

"Thought I heard someone come in," the landlord said gruffly. He was in his early fifties, retired from a local private investigation business. The man could hear a pin drop on a thick carpet.

"You're in early, Ladybro." A halo outlined his dark-skinned frame. "Everything okay?"

"Yeah." Acid boiled in her stomach. She had told him about her divorce from Kenneth and Mr. Green kept checking up on her mood. She said, "I'm just tired."

"You know, I've been thinking about you, Ladybro."

"You have?" She didn't understand the pet name he had given her when she had signed the rental contract a month ago. A lot of things Mr. Green said and did made no sense to her.

He continued, "I've had three divorces. Not easy times."

She glanced down and over the railing to offer him a smile.

He swayed from one foot to the other, swinging his arms, casually smacking the open palm on one hand into the fist of the other a few times. "Hey … ah … want to talk about it?"

"Thanks, but I just think I need—"

M-m-meow. The cat chattered and shifted in her bag.

Her heart jolted. She placed her hand into the open bag to pet the animal into a calmer state and cleared her throat. "Excuse me. I'm feeling a little tickle in my throat today."

Milton frowned, looked up at her with pinched, salt-and-pepper eyebrows. The dramatic lights emphasized his hard-edged features. "A tickle? More like a frog. Hope you haven't caught a cold." He shook his head. "They say it's going to snow tomorrow. Is the apartment warm enough?"

"Yeah." She eased one foot on the upward stair. "Everything is great with the apartment."

"Why don't you join my party? Most of the other tenants are in here." He waved a hand at the open door. "I've got some soup if you want? Meeting new friends can help you move forward, Ladybro."

"I appreciate the offer, Mr. Green."

"Yo." He threw his arms out. "Call me Milt. Mr. Green makes me feel old."

"Okay, sorry." She eased up another stair. "See you later. I just need some—"

Meow.

"Rest." She feigned a cough and hurried up the stairs to her floor.

Chapter 2

Charlie's footsteps whispered on the cold floors in her apartment. The hardwoods needed a carpet. She didn't own a radio and she recently ordered a television. She had a few pots and pans, an old dining table, a beat couch with one end table, and a king bed in the joint room.

It wasn't like her wing in her father's mansion or the large house Kenneth gained in the divorce, but it was home for now.

She had retrieved a tea set along with her other old things from deep storage and poured hot water from the hot teakettle into the dainty, ornate teacup. She looked inside her purse for the tea bags from Lance.

Little cuts marred the brown packaging where the cat tried to open it earlier. She smiled and lifted the package by its string. In doing so, the golden coin fell out of her jostled purse pocket.

The metal rang through the kitchen like a tinker's bell.

She picked the coin up from the floor and warmth sunk into her skin from the metal to her elbow. She looked at the coin. The etched words had changed. Before, when she had put the coin in her purse, the words said adopt the stray.

Now the words read: CLEAN THE CITY. 2/21.

Her surprise formed into curiosity. How did the coin work? She narrowed her eyes at it, turned it in her palm, and stroked the letters. Each time the coin had tumbled, the etched words changed.

She tossed the coin in the air and caught it. Nothing. No warmth, no glow, and no sense of change. CLEAN THE CITY remained. She dropped the coin into her pocket with her phone.

Confused, intrigued, and a little freaked out, she selected the first bag of tea at her fingertips. Her hands trembled slightly when she submerged the teabag into the hot water.

There must be a trick to the coin somehow. Something she was missing.

She settled on the couch in her small living room, careful with her hot tea, and stretched her sore legs onto the couch. She inhaled the lavender tea and sipped it. Her curiosity about the coin ebbed. Her loneliness subsided.

Her cell rang. She fished the device from her pocket and read the caller identification. "Hi, Dad."

"Hey, Sweetheart. Beth said you quit your job on Monday. How are you doing?"

Monday, the divorce from Kenneth was final. She couldn't handle working for the man anymore. "I'm okay, I guess."

"You moving back home yet?"

Tension in her stomach knotted. "No."

"You're welcome to, you know? I won't charge you rent or anything."

Peter Davies had worked hard for her. Hell, she had a million-dollar trust fund waiting for her next year, when she turned twenty-five. Growing through childhood, living life in college, nothing awful had happened to her. She couldn't tell him, or anyone, that her easy life was miserable.

There was an empty place inside, like a hole in her heart, an empty swimming pool in her soul. Day after day, month after month, the hole grew drier. She couldn't figure out how to fill it. Money wasn't the answer. Neither was marriage.

She exhaled. "What are you up to, Daddy?"

"I'm flying to Silicon Valley. I've got some business there tomorrow with Tesla Motors. I'm sorry I'm not around to support you through all of this."

"It's okay. I'll get through." She looked around at the empty apartment and closed her eyes. She wanted to believe in herself.

"I saw Kenneth in a meeting this morning. He's worried that we're going to pull our technology out of the Ghostlight Project because of the divorce."

Heat exploded in her chest, and crawled up her neck.

The Ghostlight Project was a million-dollar business arrangement. Her father had advanced technology that gave Kenneth's pyrotechnics a boost in the market. If they couldn't work together, both companies would suffer huge losses.

On the edge of her seat, she asked, "What are you going to do?"

"I don't know. There's a lot riding on this alliance already. We've got a good eight months invested, but I don't like working with a guy who's unfaithful. What's to say he won't do the same in business? If I end it now, the company may be able to recover financially after a few months."

"The business means everything to Kenneth. He'll stay committed to it. You should keep moving forward with the merger, Dad." Acid bubbled in her stomach and her skin heated.

She hated fighting for Kenneth after she had found him in bed with a flight attendant. His disloyalty. That's why she had quit her job without notice. Working for him was too much. She was done arguing his good intentions with investors when she couldn't believe them herself.

Unfortunately, this time, her father was involved. The merger was a good idea for their companies.

"I'm sorry, sweetie." Peter's tone softened. "Not the right time for this conversation. Tell me about the new place?"

"It's fine, Dad."

"I want to visit next week."

"Okay."

"I'll talk with Gina and work out the time."

"Gina?"

"My new assistant. I look forward to seeing you. I'll call again soon."

"Okay, Dad, bye."

He disconnected.

She exhaled, and relaxed her shoulders. When he visited, she hoped she had some positive news, something that supported her decisions to stay out of his house.

The phone rang again. The caller was unidentified. "Hello, this is Charlie."

"Hi, Charlie. This is Lance."

"Oh, hi, Lance."

"Sorry about the party."

"It's okay. I had fun." Despite the anxiety, she did have fun. It was a nice change from her empty life.

"I'm glad to hear that." He paused. "Did you look at the tea selection I gave you?"

"Yes, thanks, it's wonderful."

"You should come by again and I'll really show you around. They have a interesting process that I think you could appreciate."

"Okay."

"Listen, I've got to get home. I just wanted to make sure you got back okay."

"Yeah, okay, no problem. Hey, Lance?" She bit her lip afraid to speak up.

"Yeah?"

"About Zander..." She closed her eyes. She shouldn't find out more. He wasn't her type. He thought she was a home wrecker. She was just divorced on Monday. It was too early to think about getting involved with anyone.

"Did he do something to you? That—"

"No!" Heat exploded in her cheeks and she placed her free hand there to cool them. "He was nice. In fact, he walked me to the bus."

"I bet he asked you a lot of questions about me. You know, whatever he says, there are two sides to the story. If he gave you his number, you should lose it. He's not what he seems."

She lifted her eyebrows. "He seems like a nice guy."

"He's nice. He's just ... complicated."

That was twice Lance called Zander complicated. She opened her mouth to speak.

"Okay. Well. I've got to get going. Night." Lance disconnected.

She retrieved the coin from her pocket, turned it in her fingers, and sipped the tea again. Warmth eased her tension, calmed her unsettled emotions. The day wound out of her muscles.

She ran her fingers over the inscription.

A thought occurred. She rested the coin on her thigh, lifted her phone, and took a quick snapshot. She adjusted her grip and opened her Twitter account, then changed her profile picture to the coin snapshot. She tweeted her peeps for information about the coin.

...

Five blocks away from Charlie's apartment building, on the second story of Jordan's Corner Store, Rebecca Jordan answered the ringing phone on her nightstand. Her head ached and her eyes stung. She squinted at the clock. It was 3:40 a.m.

"Hello?"

"Hi, Mrs. Jordan, it's LeeAnn."

"LeeAnn?" Rebecca croaked.

LeeAnn was a reliable employee. She opened the store on the weekends, which gave Rebecca time off to sleep in. After her long night with Decker at the hospital, she needed sleep today.

LeeAnn said, "I'm not feeling well. I'm sorry to call in sick, but I just can't get away from the toilet. I think I have the flu."

Rebecca rubbed her forehead and exhaled. "Okay, LeeAnn, don't worry about it."

"I'm so sorry." LeeAnn's voice was laced with sincerity. "How's your husband?"

Rebecca rubbed at her eyes and swallowed the emotions that threaded through her exhaustion. "Every day he gets better."

LeeAnn said, "I hope he makes a full recovery."

Rebecca's firefighter husband, Decker, had fallen down a staircase while helping a neighbor move a sofa. He survived the incident but suffered severe damage to his lower back. Physically, he continued to improve. Mentally, he was struggling with the inaction.

"I hope so too. Thanks for the thought. Take care, LeeAnn. I need to get moving so I can open the store on time." She sat up in the bed and forced herself more awake.

LeeAnn coughed, moaned, and apologized again.

"LeeAnn, don't worry. I'll handle things." Rebecca couldn't see her hand in front of her face with the darkness in her bedroom. She flipped on the nightstand lamp. "Take the weekend off. Get better."

"Thanks, Mrs. Jordan." LeeAnn disconnected.

Rebecca flung the blankets off her body and slipped her feet into the jeans she had taken off forty minutes ago.

The store was a secondary income source that helped she and Decker stay involved with the community. Over the years,

21

the business had only broken even. She wasn't sure it could ever become their main income source.

Insurance covered some of the costs of his care, but she needed the store open to cover what they wouldn't.

She ran her fingers through her short hair and padded around the boxes to the sink. Downsizing to an attic studio space wasn't easy, not when their original home was a spacious three-bedroom house. She sighed and frowned. A nagging ache in her chest developed.

At least she didn't have to drive to open her store anymore.

Moments later, Rebecca headed down the staircase that ended in the back storage room of her business. She hit the switches and eased through the inventory stacks to the store itself. The weekends were her busiest days, and she couldn't afford to miss one.

Chapter 3

Charlie called the vet as soon as she woke. She made an appointment for the cat's physical tomorrow. She was surprised they had Sunday hours.

After a morning bath for both of them, she decided the cat needed a name. "Shadow" seemed fitting. She set a box of paper next to Shadow's nesting spot in the corner, hoping he was smart. "Now, you be quiet. Okay? The last thing I need is to be kicked out of this apartment."

The black-and-white tabby glanced up at her with his bright orange eyes.

She zipped her jogging coat closed. Her keys in her hand, she grabbed the magic coin and trotted out her apartment door. Her bruised knees from the fall on the cement last night were sore, but nothing to cry about.

She needed a good run. Nothing eased her stress more.

The cat had added something different to her life too. For good or bad yet, she wasn't sure. She figured she would play along with the coin. She didn't have a better plan for finding happiness at the moment. Maybe she would discover something else.

On the stair landing she smiled at Marie Young, a neighbor. "Hello."

"Hello, Charlie." Marie puffed. "You going running?"

"I usually run every morning." Charlie shifted to the side for the older woman to pass. "I'm a little late today."

"I suspect everyone is late today. Out last night partying. I know. I was young once too. Young and stupid. Made for a nice shop at the market today, though." Marie shifted a small bag to her shoulder and pointed at Charlie's hands. "Hives?"

Charlie nodded. She rubbed at her skin. "They come out when I'm worried."

"A good run'll be great for you then." When Marie smiled, the corners of her eyes wrinkled. She brushed back her smoky curls. "Just be careful. It's starting to snow."

"Yes, ma'am." Charlie headed down the stairs.

She hurried out of the apartment building. Cold air pinched her cheeks and tightened her lungs. Large, heavy flakes of snow fell on her shoulders. Overhead, the gray clouds moved slowly with a light glow behind them. People strolled along the street and cars passed unnoticed.

She lost herself in the rhythm of her splashing footsteps on the slush-covered sidewalk.

Forty minutes later, she paused to catch her breath.

Steam from her mouth mingled with the dense air around her. This spot usually had potted flowers beside the bench. Today, the pots were gone and the street corner seemed dreary without them. A thin coat of snow sat on the surface under her feet.

She stretched her tight thigh muscles and glanced around the four-way stop where classic brick buildings lined the unusually empty street. She supposed Maria was right about Friday party recovery. Coupled with the snow, it made people stay inside.

A wrapper floated in the air. Charlie remembered the words on the coin to clean the city. She shrugged, jogged to the trash, and snatched it up. A half-block later, on her way home, she tossed the trash in a street bin.

Charlie fished the golden coin from her pocket and flipped. It flew into the air as if in slow motion, catching the light as it turned. When it finally touched down in the palm of her hand, the metal warmed her closed fingers and a tingling sensation traveled up her arm to her elbow.

Her fingers rubbed the warm metal. She turned the coin in her hands. Besides the crude quality, it seemed like other coins she had seen before. It was heavy, detailed, and real. She opened her palm and read the words.

Sing in public 3/21.

"What?" She stared at the words for a moment. "I don't sing."

She glanced around and tucked the coin in her pocket. A gust of cold wind chilled her to the bone and the snow thickened. She spotted Jordan's Corner Store and hurried inside for warmth.

She veered toward a magazine display and picked up the local newspaper. Opposite the display, there were small tables beside the front windows. The checkout counter was behind the

Judy Dawn

magazines and a blonde woman talked with a tall man dressed in a thick parka.

Charlie eased into one of the chairs at a table near the front of the store.

"Thanks for salting the parking lot," the blonde said to the tall man. "I'm sorry I can't pay you in cash today."

"I understand," the man said with a handsome smile. "I'll open a tab for you. I'm not worried about it. I've got to pick up some snacks before I go, though." He started for the back of the store.

"Take anything you need." The woman shifted behind the counter.

The tall man admired some shovels on the wall and disappeared behind a stocked shelf. The woman hovered over a book on the counter, her eyebrows knit, and scribbled in the book with a red pen.

Charlie knew that look from years of accounting: The store was in financial trouble.

The other store tables were empty, soft music played overhead. A mix of cooked beef, chicken, and pork filled the air from the large machines near the far wall. Charlie glanced at the newspaper in her hands and turned a few pages.

Her mind racing with titles of songs she knew, Her mouth dried and she trembled at the idea of singing in public. She wasn't a singer. She didn't have the talent. In high school, her choir coach told her not to sing loudly because she threw everyone off-key.

The idea of opening her mouth made her stomach curdle. Her hives deepened in color with her heightened anxiety and she scratched at her neck. She couldn't catch a full breath.

Singing in public was crazy.

The wind whistled through the windows. Charlie couldn't shake the strange feeling in her gut that the weather was in cohorts with the coin's power.

Power? Now, she was crazy. Coins didn't have power. Magic didn't exist. Yet, the words on the coin changed with each flip and she couldn't explain it.

She focused on the newspaper. A small headline caught her attention. She started to read the article about resolutions: *You want a change. You have to do it. Change comes with risk.*

Charlie wanted a change. She had moved into her own apartment because she needed to stand by herself and find some new friends. Unsure of what would make her happy, she risked her security. What more would it take?

A bell on the door jingled and a strange man entered the store.

He yanked off his hat, smiled at the woman behind the counter, and grabbed *Wired* magazine from the display. He settled at a table in front of Charlie.

Charlie fished the coin from her pocket and studied the etching again.

Change comes with risk. In this case, the risk was embarrassment. No, no, no, she couldn't do it. She hugged the coin and made a wish.

She glanced around the store noting the small crowd of three. Florescent lights above flickered near the back corner. When she looked at the coin again, the gold sparkled and warmth coursed through her hand to her wrist.

None of these people knew her. She wasn't likely to see them again.

On a surge of adrenaline, she stood and opened her mouth. Before she realized what she was doing, words spewed from her lips: *"The weather outside is frightful, but the fire is so delightful, and since we've got no place to go, let it snow, let it snow, let it snow."*

Her heart climbed into her chest when she considered the wide-eyed strangers. The man at the table in front of her turned to face her with his mouth dropped open. And the woman behind the counter put her hand on her lips, grimacing, as if she had tasted something awful.

The tall guy stared at her like she had three heads.

Charlie swallowed, glanced at the coin, and flipped it in the air. It landed in her hand with the same words on it. Her stomach knotted and she refrained from moaning. Instead she continued: *"Oh, it doesn't show signs of stopping, and I've brought some corn for popping—"*

"Since the lights are turned way down low, let it snow, let it snow, let it snow." The voice of an angel joined her and made Charlie sound better. The woman behind the counter sauntered out, increasing her volume.

"The fire is slowly dying," the tall man's low baritone joined the song. He turned toward the woman at the counter. *"My dear, we're still good-bye-ing."*

"But as long as you love me so..." Charlie quieted her voice to meld within the better two singers and her shoulders dropped. Anxiety shifted into relief. She smiled through the last of the song as it ended on a beautiful, harmonized, uplifting note.

The man at the table set down his phone and clapped. "Well done!"

"Thank you." The blonde bowed and returned to the counter.

The tall man laughed, waved at the blonde, and headed out the door. "I'll see you later."

Charlie sat, caught her breath, and closed the newspaper. Her trembling subsided. The thrill of overcoming her fear of singing coursed through her body with a wave of joy and reward. She didn't think she had the guts to overcome that fear, ever. And she had just done it.

She wanted to cheer, jump, and dance around. She didn't want to push her luck.

Containing her excitement, she flipped the coin without a second thought. The gold caught the light and sparkled as if tiny diamonds were embedded in the metal. When it landed in her hand, a warm sensation zinged up to her elbow.

She bit her lower lip and read her next task: GIVE HOMELESS COFFEE. 4/21.

She tucked the coin in her pocket. Her energy high, she hurried to the coffee pot. She didn't see any disposable cups, so she grabbed two handmade ceramic cups and paid. She smiled at the blonde behind the counter and read her nametag. "Thanks for singing along, Rebecca!"

Rebecca smiled. "It was fun."

"Are you a professional singer?"

"No, I just love to do it. Music lifts my spirit."

Charlie nodded understanding. "Well, it did that for me today. Thanks again."

"Anytime. Stay warm out there and come back to see us."

"I will." Charlie elbowed through the door, into the cold weather, and glanced around the street. Rebecca was nice. Charlie hoped she was wrong about the store being in financial trouble.

Charlie's foot slipped on a patch of ice, but she righted herself without trouble while she searched the street. She figured the snow kept most of the homeless nestled in their boxes.

She peeked around the corner of an alley and spotted a woman with a shopping cart hunkered down beside a Dumpster.

Charlie had never thought of giving a homeless person anything. She had always walked by them without making eye contact. They kind of scared her, like clowns or aliens in horror movies, in a way she couldn't justify. She trembled with her thoughts. Heat exploded throughout her body.

Maybe it was the facelessness, the mask of a desperate stranger, that worried her more. People did strange things when they were desperate.

Charlie glanced at the cups in her hands. They weren't going to serve themselves and the thing she did in the coffee shop went well. This should go well too.

She inhaled and the cool air refreshed her will. Were all homeless people desperate? Her father had put that idea in her head. Like everything else her father had told her, Charlie wanted to find out about it on her own. She understood what she was about to do was foolish.

Setting aside doubt, Charlie straightened her spine and took a step.

It seemed darker and colder with the tall walls bookending her body. Snowflakes floated at random without a breeze to lead them. Her heartbeat raced, her body shook, and her mouth dried.

Charlie approached the homeless stranger. She tried to understand the stranger's words, but couldn't make anything out of them. "Excuse me."

The woman looked at her as if she had cursed. The homeless woman's face was covered in dirt and bruises. She wore

28

a hole-riddled stocking cap over snarled black locks of hair. "What?"

"Would you like a cup of coffee?"

"What'd you put 'nit?"

"It's black. Fresh from the corner store."

The woman placed a hand on her chest. "Well, la-de-da. We're drinking high today."

"Do you like coffee?" Charlie sipped the warm liquid to show her intentions were pure. "I was just out for a run and I saw you. It's cold. Would you keep me company while I drink my coffee?"

The woman's eyebrows rose. "She wants us to keep her company." She giggled like a schoolgirl. "Me?"

"Yes. If you've got time." Charlie offered the cup. "For you."

"For us?" The woman's rag-covered hands hugged the cup. Her green eyes turned pink and tears pooled. "For me?"

"My name is Charlie, what's yours?"

"Dottie, our name is Dottie." The homeless woman lifted the cup to her nose. It shook in her hands. "Smells good."

"That's a good name." Charlie swallowed the absurdity of her fear. The lady was different, not dangerous. "The snow is beautiful, don't you think?"

"It's cold." Dottie's voice dropped. She sipped the coffee. Tears seeped from the corners of her eyes, cleaning a path on her dirtied cheeks. "We ran outside. We didn't care 'bout the cold. We should have had coffee earlier. It would have helped."

Charlie wanted to know what Dottie was talking about, but kept the conversation light. "A friend of mine warned me about the snow today."

"A friend, she says," Dottie repeated. She patted a spot on the ground. "Does she want to sit with us?"

Charlie eased to the ground. Melted snow seeped into the butt of her exercise pants. She ignored the cooling sensation. "Thanks for taking the time."

"She thanks us." Dottie snorted. "So nice."

Male voices echoed from down the street. Charlie figured the boys were playing in the snow. She glanced in their direction. Two young men laughed and joked when they crossed the alley entrance. Two more boys ran behind to catch up.

"No," Dottie whispered, "he always finds us."

Charlie studied the fear in the woman's blue eyes. "I think we'll be okay. They can't see us behind the dumpster."

"No, they found us." Dottie struggled to stand.

Charlie's heart fell to her stomach. She wished she could ease the other woman's anxiety. "Wait, it's probably okay."

Dottie dropped her coffee, the mug broke, and she grabbed the handle of her shopping cart. "Nice lady, we need to run."

"Ho, ho, there she is!" The boys entered the alley and marched toward Dottie and Charlie.

The four young men were dressed in winter wear. The two in front seemed like brothers, with matching wide faces. There was also a redhead and a boy in a brown leather jacket.

"There's the old lady. And what do we have here? A friend?"

"Run," Dottie commanded.

Charlie stood, careful with the hot liquid in her cup. "Do you know these young men?"

"It's him. It's him. We've got to run." Dottie yanked at Charlie's elbow. "Go. Time to go. Run. Please."

One of the teenagers yelled, "She remembers something."

"See, Sage," the redheaded boy smacked his friend's shoulder. "Beat her enough and she'll remember. We're brilliant. We'll make millions with our methods."

"Ohhh," Dottie covered her face with her palms and shrunk her wobbly body into a ball on the ground. "We should have run. We should have run. Too late."

Charlie had never been in a fight before. She had attended many hostile negotiations with her father and he had shown her to never quit. At times, the bark was worse than the bite.

Her hands were unstable, the blood raced in her veins. Fear pumped her energy.

The taller, wide-chinned boy in front approached her. He reached out a hand.

Charlie swatted it away. "Back off."

The group laughed. "Look at her. She's so strong but she's trembling. Hey, old lady, you got a new bodyguard?"

Dottie whimpered behind Charlie.

"You should have picked someone with more muscle." The teen taunted. "Look at those little—"

"Listen, you look like smart boys. Why don't you just walk away?" Charlie strained the authority in her voice. "I don't want to hurt you."

The boys exchanged glances, and burst out laughing. "Hurt us?"

She smiled at their amusement. And threw her hot coffee in the face of the nearest boy.

"Damn." He yelled and swung a fist into her gut.

Air rushed from her lungs. Her muscles cramped. She fell to her knees. A hit to the eye distracted her from her urge to throw up, and she nosedived to the ground. Behind her, Dottie screamed. Pain clouded Charlie's thoughts.

Charlie couldn't make heads or tails of anything. Her body shut down from the horrendous pain. She lay on the cold asphalt as chaos exploded around her.

Sirens? Voices?

She shook her head, blinked out of the daze, and realized the police were there. Her thoughts buzzed incoherently. Someone touched her shoulder. She jumped. "No!"

"Easy." A shadow blocked the world from her senses and a calm voice said, "Take it easy. We've got an ambulance on the way. You're going to be okay."

"What about—" Charlie groaned when she shifted positions.

"I know it hurts. I've been on the receiving end of a couple of fists a time or two." The uniformed policeman squatted next to her. "You'll be okay."

She nodded, exhaled a painful breath, and looked at him. Her legs were cold. Sitting on the ground, she shivered.

The policeman tenderly squeezed her shoulder. "What are you doing in this alley?"

She shook her head, righted her attention. "I was giving a cup of coffee to a homeless woman." She glanced around. "Is she okay?"

"Yeah, she's okay." The policeman gestured to someone over her shoulder.

Charlie looked in that direction, her neck shot a small pain to her ear. She winced when she spotted more uniformed police arresting the teenage boys. Her homeless friend was talking with a female officer.

Charlie exhaled. "She's okay."

"You said you were giving a cup of coffee to a homeless woman?"

Charlie looked at the officer again. Her perceptions were slightly unfocused, but he seemed familiar. "Yes," she answered his question. "Then these guys came around the corner. Dottie was afraid. She told me to run." She attempted to stand.

"You didn't," he finished for her and helped her up.

She nodded, exhaled the pain from her body, and realized that moving eased her cramped muscles. She hugged her ribs and straightened.

The police officer helped her gain her balance with his strong hold on her elbows. He asked, "Do you remember what happened next?"

"There were four boys all together. They called the homeless lady 'old woman,' like they knew her or something." Charlie nodded to the officer. She gently pushed his hands away from her arms while she tested the strength of her legs. "One was named Sage, I think."

A little more stable, her fingers gripped the cup, she continued, "Then I threw coffee in the face of the one who tried to grab me and everything gets a little fuzzy."

"Do you remember what the guy who tried to grab you looked like?"

"Yeah." She shifted her sore jaw. One eye wasn't working right. She gingerly fingered the swelling in her face. "I'm glad you're arresting those boys."

"You want to press charges?"

She read the cup: SOME DAYS JUST AREN'T WORTH PUTTING ON A BRA.

"Ma'am?"

Charlie refocused her attention on the policeman.

He stood a head taller than her five-foot-six. His shoulders filled out the uniform well. She had seen one set of shoulders about that width before. Short dark-brown hair, styled with a conservative cut, matched his thick eyebrows. He had incredibly long lashes framing hazel eyes with flecks of gold. His jawline and naturally tanned skin reminded her of ... someone.

"Have we met before?" She studied his full lips.

"Sorry, I don't think so." The officer smiled, stood straighter. "Did you want to file charges?"

She couldn't shake the familiarity. "Yes. Yes, I do."

"Okay, come with me and we'll get this all sorted out."

...

Zander Sharp sat at the desk in his apartment's study area, hair wet from a late morning shower. He thought the warm water would ease his tense muscles about his current undercover job, but he was wrong. He glanced at his watch expecting a call from his ASAC. The boss wanted a status report and he had nothing new to tell.

His stomach knotted while the pictures of his family flashed on his laptop screensaver. His mother, rest her soul, had died of an overdose. Zander had two brothers. When their mother died, the brothers were housed in separate foster homes. Zander hadn't seen his brothers for years. He had attempted to find them. Unfortunately, time and computer viruses had complicated the records.

Once he had put an ad in *The Seattle Times*, including old pictures of his brothers. And ad in the paper. He closed his eyes and exhaled. That's where he saw the woman at the shop last night. Not in *The Seattle Times*, but somewhere else.

She was related to an up-and-coming business tycoon. She had gotten married a while back, if he remembered right. Maybe a year and a half back.

His fingers flew over the keys as he searched the Internet. A dozen articles about new marriages flashed in front of him, then he lifted his hands when he saw her chestnut hair with a white veil frame. She was in the Mercer Island news for a month.

"I'll be damned."

Zander read the article about pampered Charlotte Davies, who got hitched to a pyrotechnic engineer named Kenneth Oliver. They had met during a business merger between her father's high-tech think tank and the pyrotechnics design outfit.

Zander pressed his lips and rubbed the ache between his temples. "I hope you're not deeply involved with Lance Dixon, Princess. That would be a shame all the way around."

He looked at his watch again. Then out the window. He missed the sun. He had worked on this case for over a month now, and it was one of the longest cases he had investigated. The phone rang and he answered.

"Hey, Sharp, how's your morning going?" Assistant Special Agent in Charge Elvis "EJ" James seemed cheerful.

"It's going, sir." Zander carried the phone with him to the kitchen and grabbed the empty coffee pot. He filled it with water and started a new brew. "How's the family?"

EJ was an okay guy outside of the DEA office. Married with three children, the ASAC had gray hair and a wide face. His aged voice reflected years of hard undercover work, like Zander's current field mission.

"The kids are enjoying the snow." He chuckled.

Zander smiled and flipped on the coffee pot.

EJ cleared his throat. "Let's get this report done so I can go make a snowman. What have you got?"

Lance Dixon was out on probation from distributing methamphetamine over six months ago. Dixon's wife had bailed him out with their life savings. When Dixon got a new job to recover the bail money, Zander landed the same job. Zander stuck to the dealer with the hope of locating the meth lab or the group that owned the meth lab.

"Last night, Lance had me deliver a package to a woman named Charlie Davies. I didn't get a chance to look inside the package."

"Charlie Davies seems like a name I've heard before."

"I looked her up this morning. She's the daughter of a high-tech tycoon on Mercer Island. He's involved a number of million-dollar projects. She was married last year. There's not much after." He grabbed a cup and poured the fresh brew. The first sip tingled along his tongue.

"Maybe he gave her a sample."

"I'm not sure. I talked with her a little bit, but I didn't get much from her."

Zander shook his head even though EJ couldn't see him. He couldn't argue facts, but there was something about her, a vulnerability that sat in his gut like bad cheese. He rubbed his right shoulder out of habit. An old football injury he had received in high school, ruining his hopes to play college ball.

"I'll have a background check done on her."

"Yes, sir." Zander studied his coffee in thought. "Run one on the husband too."

"Good idea." EJ exhaled. "Is there anything else?"

He hated saying, "No, sir."

There was a pause before EJ said, "Well, the kids are pulling at my arms. I've got to go. Did you get your anniversary gift yet?"

"Anniversary?" Zander looked at the phone.

"Remember, I invited you to the Chief's fifteenth anniversary dinner party. It'll be good for you to make some new contacts. It's likely you'll have to transfer after this investigation. Everyone in Dixon's network knows you now."

Zander nodded and rubbed his shoulder. As much as he liked the job, he hated the travel. He was in his early thirties without a family or a home. After he tied up this investigation, he wanted a month off to search for his brothers. He would cross that subject with his boss when the time came.

"I haven't got a gift yet."

"You'd better get something nice. That's an order, Agent."

"Will do, sir. Have fun in the snow." Snow days were slow. The city budget didn't account for snowplows. They only needed them once or twice a year.

Zander glanced at the new voicemail he received while on the phone with his boss. Without snowplows, most of the businesses were closed. He listened to the voicemail about the Green Leaf and Brew not opening today and dug out some eggs from the fridge. Maybe he would visit his father. He wondered what old Milt had been up to lately.

...

Charlie glanced around the narrow lobby again. A wall of glass with a decent view of a non-operational fountain. Commercial art that blended into the wall. A greeting desk where phones rang and a person's non-remarkable voice mixed with music.

Her chest pinged at the memory of her bedroom view in her father's house. Her room there was bigger than her apartment put together. Seattle rained most of the year and the benefit was lush vegetation. Her favorite place on the grounds was the rose garden outside her window.

She glanced around again, sighed, and dug out her phone from her pocket. She quickly accessed her settings to turn on notifications from her Twitter account, so she could receive real-time replies about her earlier inquiry about the coin.

Charlie looked up. The man she waited for smiled at the woman behind the greeting desk and headed toward Charlie.

Officer Corbin Black was polite. His kindheartedness was reassuring. After a day of violence, out of her comfort zone, she craved security and peace.

When he asked Charlie if he could drive her home from the precinct after she had filed charges against her attackers, she agreed without hesitation. The idea of riding the bus with bruised ribs and a tired mind didn't appeal to her. She smiled while he held the precinct door open for her on the way out of the building.

He wore a V-neck sweater, black slacks, and loafers, and his sincere smile warmed her disposition.

"Thank you for driving me from the hospital to the station, Corbin." He had asked her to drop the formalities after the hour they spent together at the hospital. She added, "Now, the ride home. I'll bet you had better plans for evening off."

"Actually, I didn't." He followed her into a thick, evening mist. Snow had melted into a sticky slush on the ground. Corbin asked, "I'm starving. Do you feel up to grabbing some Japanese food before I drop you off? My treat."

She glanced down at her dried, dirty jogging suit and frowned. "I'm not really dressed for going out."

"I know a place. You'll be fine. Heck, I'll even splurge for a Coke if you want one!" His chuckle brought a smile to her lips.

Despite her tired mood, she needed food and she liked Corbin's company. "Sure. Okay. But I'd rather have a vanilla shake."

"A shake it is." He laughed and used his hand on her lower back to casually steer her through the tiny City Hall Park, where she admired a silver sculpture.

She maneuvered the stairs to the main walk and across the busy street. A few times he shielded her body with his when strangers hustled by them. His calm, protective demeanor eased her worry.

In the center of a small parking lot was the restaurant. "I stop here often," Corbin said. "We'll get a table in back so you won't have to worry about anyone looking at that black eye."

Charlie winced at the reminder of her beating. She would rather file away the horrid experience and move forward.

But she thought about her foolishness, entering that alley alone. She learned that she needed some self-defense lessons. Her stomach knotted. She had walked away with bruises. Next time she might not get so lucky.

Inside, a beautiful, dark-haired hostess smiled at Corbin. "Ah, hello, sir. Would you like your regular table?"

"One in the back, please, Mei."

"Yes." She picked up two menus and started through the semi-busy restaurant. Tables with white covers scattered throughout the room. The lights were low and dark wood colors lent warmth to the ambiance. A savory aroma reminded Charlie that she hadn't eaten in a few hours.

The phone buzzed in her pocket when she slid into the booth. She settled the bag from the hospital with her mug and medicine. She dug out her cell phone and smiled. She received a few tweets about the coin.

> *The image isn't clear. Do you have other pictures with details?*@ConCoin
> *It looks like a commemorative coin.*@ProTrader

*I don't recognize the template. It's not
something mass-produced.@CCI*

She clicked her phone off. "So, what's your favorite
thing here?"

"Spring rolls." He opened the menu. "I don't see
shakes."

She laughed, comforted her bruised ribs with her arm,
and said, "That's okay. Maybe next time."

He glanced up from the menu and the candlelight
defined the gold specks in his hazel-green eyes. "Will there be a
next time?"

She hoped the low light covered her blush. "You're
being very nice to me."

"You've been through a lot this week." He leaned back
in the seat. "You got a divorce on Monday."

"How did you know that?"

"Public record." He smiled. "I'm good at my job,
Charlie."

"Oh." She blushed again.

"Is that why you moved off Mercer Island?"

"Have you ever been married, Corbin?"

"I came close once." He rubbed the sandy stubble on his
jaw and glanced around. He chuckled morbidly, and waved a
dismissive hand. There was a hint of agitation in his gaze. "They
all say I'm married to my work."

She rested her hands in her lap. "I understand. I've been
called a workaholic too." She placed her fingers on her forehead,
rubbed, and hissed at the flare of pain of her black eye.

Corbin reached for her hand, set it on the table under his.
"That's not going to help your headache." The sincerity in his
eyes and softness of his tone went a long way toward easing her
discomfort.

The pain in her eye subsided to a dull ache.

Craving a connection, she twisted her palm so her
fingers could rub Corbin's knuckles. His skin was silky under her
caress. "Are you happy?"

"That's a big question, Charlie."

She laughed. "I think the medicine is getting to me. I guess, I just, have you ever felt like there's something missing in your life? Like you just don't matter."

Corbin's gaze filled with understanding and some of the tension in her chest eased. "I think everyone feels like they disappear sometimes even when they're right in the center of things."

Charlie pulled back her hand to drink from her water, then ordered a Coke. The soft sound of a flute accompanied by stringed instruments filled a moment of silence at the table.

The aches in her body made her wonder why she went against instinct?

Charlie retrieved the coin from her pocket and studied the golden shine.

The coin hadn't forced her.

There was something else, another reason, for her unusual behavior. When she was in the alley, she had enjoyed talking with Dottie. The idea of making Dottie's day a little nicer made Charlie feel better too.

The warmth from the coin heated her palm. She rested her elbows on the table and looked at Corbin reading the menu. "How did you know what was happening in the alley? I didn't see any police cars on the street."

Corbin focused on her. "The corner store owner, I think her name was Rebecca, saw you go into the alley. She saw the gang go there too and decided to call it in."

"Thank goodness." Charlie nodded. She rubbed the coin with the pad of her thumb. "How long have you been a police officer?"

"My mother moved me and my brothers to Seattle when we were teenagers. We were separated into foster homes and I joined the force at twenty-three. That was ten years ago."

Charlie nodded.

He closed the menu. "What are you going to have?"

She glanced at the coin in her palm, smiled, and pushed the menu away. She decided she had enough heavy thinking for one day. "You know what? I'll let you order for me. I don't have any allergies, but I'm not into spicy foods."

He chuckled. His wide smile exposed one chipped tooth on the bottom row in his mouth. "I'll be sure to keep that in mind."

She settled back. "Did you always know you wanted to be a cop?"

"Not really." He leaned back too. "But, I want to find my brothers and I figured being a cop could help me. The job suits me. I feel rewarded when I help people. I like being a part of the community." His features softened as he relaxed. "What about you? Do you always give coffee to the homeless?"

She laughed, shook her head. "Today has been … a whirlwind of new stuff."

He leaned forward. "Tell me about it."

She placed the coin on the table.

He lifted the coin, turned it between his long fingers, and studied the impressions.

"I took the adventure because of that coin."

He flicked his hand and the coin was gone. "What coin?"

Her heartbeat stuttered. "What? Where is it?"

He moved his hand to her chest, reached into the collar of her jogging jacket, and showed her the coin as it reappeared in her palm. He spun it on the table. "It's a trick my brother taught me."

"Maybe you could teach me a few tricks." Heat flamed in her cheeks. "I mean." She exhaled. "That didn't come out right."

He smiled and shrugged.

In the awkward silence, she drank some cool water.

He cleared his throat. "So, tell me about this coin. "

How could she say the coin was magical? She barely accepted it herself and she had seen it work firsthand. "Things happen when I flip it."

"Do they?" He tossed it in the air.

She held her breath.

He caught it, looked at the inscription, and showed it to her. "Still says GIVE HOMELESS COFFEE."

She took the coin back. "There's a number that counts down with each flip. See. Right there, the little four-slash-twenty-one. Maybe it doesn't change owners until all the flips are done."

His smile stretched and he folded his arms. "Flip it. Let me see it change."

"Are you challenging me?"

"Yeah."

What if it didn't work? Sweat popped on her forehead and her chest gripped with anxiety. A deep breath, a silent count to three....

She tossed the coin in the air.

Chapter 4

Funny thing: Changing lifestyle usually meant changing friends. Not by choice but by social surroundings. People grouped and lived within a like culture. In high school, they were called cliques. Today, they were called social networks.

When Charlie moved from a mansion to lower-income housing, the prospect of losing good friends weighed heavy on her shoulders. With life upside down, confused, and going nowhere, she needed an understanding friend.

She welcomed Bethany Hardgrave into the scattered boxes of her new apartment.

Best friends since college, they used to travel together and Beth had witnessed Charlie's worst moments. Beth's surprised reaction to Charlie's bruises from the alleyway attack was expected.

"Are you okay?" Beth gently hugged Charlie.

"Yeah, I'll be fine." She wasn't sure, actually, but she didn't want to worry Beth. "The doctors said I needed a few days' rest."

"Who did this to you?" Beth inched a few feet away.

"Come inside and I'll tell you all about it." Charlie stepped beside the open door and got a whiff of lilacs. Her tense muscles relaxed a little. "Did you get some new perfume?"

"I bought some body wash the last time I was in London."

"When was that?"

"Two days ago." Beth stood in the center of the great room and turned in a circle.

Great room. The thought made Charlie smile while she closed the door. The only thing that was great about the room was her father didn't own it. "Would you like some tea?"

"Why did you choose this place?" Beth looked up and down at the aged wallpaper and antique fixtures.

"The low rent helps me save money."

"You don't have to save money." Beth's light green eyes locked stares with Charlie. "Unless something happened in the divorce settlement I don't know about. Did Kenneth get his claws into your trust fund?"

"No. Besides, I can't touch that until next year."

"Well, you've got a good reputation in the industry. You can get any accountant job you want. Have you been having troubles finding one?"

"Yes." Charlie told small lies well. It was the bigger ones that got her into trouble.

Truth was, she had trained for years to take a spot within the corporate leadership bracket. The more people she had met at that level, the more she realized she didn't want to become one of those people. They were lifeless droids punching numbers for companies they didn't care about, that didn't care about them.

It didn't matter how much money they made or how secure they were financially. They never smiled. Meaningless droids. She didn't want to be like them anymore.

Her self-discovery had wilted her optimism. It was hard admitting to herself she had wasted years of studying something in college that she couldn't stomach in practice. Without work, she had nothing.

She shrugged off a sharp stab from her sadness. "What about that tea?" Charlie limped to the kitchen and turned on the pot full of water. "My place isn't so bad."

"If you need help finding a job, I'm sure your father could help you make some new connections."

Charlie's gut knotted. "I want to keep my father out of this."

"Why?" Beth rested her forearms on the bar.

Charlie faced Beth's inquisitive expression. "I need to learn how to struggle."

"I don't understand. People go through life wishing they didn't need to struggle."

"You're talking about people wanting money."

"Yes."

Charlie picked two lemon zest teabags and placed them in the waiting cups. She reread the funny quote, SOME DAYS JUST AREN'T WORTH PUTTING ON A BRA, and poured the hot water into the cups then handed one to Beth.

"Funny mug. Not really your style." Beth smiled.

"I picked it up the other day at a corner store."

They settled at the small dining room table and Charlie continued, "People who wish they had money struggle with not having money. They don't struggle with life. They already have a purpose and friends. They have a direction. If they had money, they would know what to do with it to improve their dreams. I haven't struggled. I have the money, but I don't know what to do with it. How can I use it to improve my life?"

"Are you saying you have no dreams?" Beth leaned back in the chair.

Charlie threw out her hands. "I have money, but nothing else."

Beth pressed her thin lips in a line. She scrunched her painted eyebrows together trying to understand. "You have a loving father, good friends, a great career."

"But I'm unhappy." Charlie smoothed her thumb over the handle on the cup.

"Well," Beth's tone changed. She shook her head and exhaled. "I never understand. You've always seen the worst of things even when they're good. Location doesn't really matter. I guess arguing is futile at this point. You're always going to live in misery despite all the good that surrounds you."

"What are you—?"

Someone knocked.

"Who is it?" Charlie stood, hurried to the door, and waited for an answer.

"Milt. I had to sign for a delivery to you and decided to bring it up."

"Just leave it by the door." Charlie's heart hammered against her chest. She looked around for Shadow.

Beth, sensing Charlie's anxiety, stood. "What's going on?"

Charlie whispered, "The cat. I can't have the cat in this apartment."

"Cat?" Beth glanced around on the floor.

"It's big." Milt's bold voice projected through the door. "I'm not sure you can pick it up on your own."

"Uh, okay, just a minute." Charlie knelt on her hands and knees, looking for the cat. She groaned as her movements irritated her bruised ribs.

"Hey," Beth's loud whisper drew Charlie's attention. Beth held the cat up. Charlie signaled to put the cat in her room. Beth closed the bedroom door as Charlie opened the front door.

Charlie brushed at a wayward hair in her eyes trying to cover the blush from her sudden exertion. "Sorry for making you wait, Milt."

"That's all right, Ladybro," Milt greeted as he walked in, hefting a box. His heavy, booted steps echoed off the bare walls. "Where do you want this?"

She initially wanted it in the bedroom, but with the cat in there, she pointed at the far wall. "Over there. Thanks, Milt. You didn't have to do that."

He looked at Charlie and his easy expression tightened. She couldn't tell if he was angry or frustrated. His brown eyes narrowed, crooked nose pinched, and his full lips tensed.

"What happened to your face?"

Charlie stepped back at his accusatory tone. "Excuse me."

"Sorry." Milt straightened, shoved his hands in his front pockets, and rolled his head on his thick neck as if he were establishing personal control. He said, "I mean, you're beautiful as always. I just noticed the bruises and it got me all riled up. If someone is mistreatin' ya, I can help ya with that."

"No." Charlie shook her head and lifted an open palm. "I just got into a fight."

She quickly told him the story.

"What were you doing in the alley?" asked Beth, who had returned to the living room.

"I gave a cup of coffee to a homeless woman." Charlie didn't want to go into further detail. How could she explain the magic coin in such a short amount of time? She decided to distract everyone from the story. "Anyway, looks like I got my new TV. I ordered it a few days ago."

"Is that what this is?" Milt looked at the large box. "Ya got any tools to install it?"

"Tools?" Charlie lifted her eyebrows with her surprise. She didn't realize she needed tools to get the TV to work. "No."

He rubbed his chin and nodded at Beth then held out a hand in greeting. "Hi, I'm Milt Green, the superintendent of the building."

"I'm Beth." The two shook hands.

"I'm sorry, guys, I didn't think. Where is my brain?" Charlie touched the cut on her sore forehead.

"Probably still in the alley." Beth smiled.

"Now, let me see this." Milt moved to the box, squatted down, and looked at the details written on the side. "It shouldn't be to hard to install. I could do it for you. I've got the tools to put the mounting bracket on the wall."

Beth settled on the couch. Her signature perfume spread in the air. She wore tights under an overlong shirt, the perfect shade of gold to compliment her lemon-colored hair. She smiled at Milt's backside, then raised her eyebrows at Charlie. Beth said, "I like the view you have here, Charlie."

Charlie's skin heated at Beth's nerve.

Milt stood. He looked at Beth, then the tips of Milt's ears turned black cherry.

"I'd appreciate the help, Milt." Charlie tried to smooth the awkwardness.

"I've been meanin' to install a new showerhead for your bathroom. While I'm installin' the TV—" He took a few steps toward the bedroom, the only access to her bathroom.

Charlie hurried to block the door. Out of breath from her sudden movement, she swayed on weak knees and whispered, "No."

"Take it easy, Ladybro." Milt gripped her elbow tenderly. He escorted her to the couch and helped her settle in. "Ya got to let your body heal."

"I just don't want you to go into my room right now. It's a mess."

"All right. I'll go get my tools so I can hang the TV for ya. I'll do the showerhead another time." He hurried to the door and closed it after him.

Charlie exhaled. She glanced at Beth, the silence stretched.

Beth folded her arms and didn't look away.

"What?"

Beth's eyebrows drew together again. "I can't believe this. You're fighting in alley, nursing bruises, breaking rules by hiding a cat from your landlord, and covered in hives that are not going to go away easily. That color of red means months of calamine. I'm worried about you."

Beth's earnestness melted the last of Charlie's bravery. Her tight control disintegrated and tears burst from her eyes. Her body exploded with heat from the rush of emotion. She couldn't catch her breath. Charlie sobbed. "You're right. Everything is a mess. My apartment. My job. My life."

Beth hugged her. The warmth soothed Charlie a little. "Well, you said you wanted a struggle." Beth lightened her voice.

"Yeah." A morbid chuckle escaped Charlie's throat. She inhaled Beth's sweet perfume while she silently reminded herself of why she had left Mercer Island.

"Why are you putting yourself through all of this pain?" Beth brushed Charlie's hair from her face.

Charlie inhaled, wiped her tears, and looked at Beth with more control. "I'd rather feel the pain than nothing at all."

Beth's shoulders dropped. She exhaled and settled back to study Charlie. Beth's angular features softened into angelic beauty when she smiled. "I have the sudden urge to move in here with you. Someone has to make sure you don't kill yourself."

A knock came at the door. Milt poked his head inside. "I'm back."

...

Clouds opened up in a spring downpour, drenching Rebecca Jordan from head to shoulder. Her chest constricted as emotion built up in her mind and body. Tears cascaded down her cheeks. Her hands shook as she locked the door to her car. She thought the drive would give her the time she needed, but she entered the front doors of the hospital still unsure on how to approach her husband.

She needed to tell Decker that she permanently closed the store this morning. The money wasn't there for medical bills and business costs. Even though the injury happened on the job, he hadn't been on an official call. They refused to pay him disability and the medical insurance barely helped financially. To top it off, he had been forced to quit or be fired for negligence and bad judgment.

One of them needed a new job. Decker wouldn't be able to work anywhere until he was on his feet again. The injury to his back would limit him. Spending most of her time on the store, she didn't have a big resumé.

What was she going to do? They had counted on the store for his retirement. Now, they had no future. It was all her fault. She was silly to spend so much time on such a big risk when she was young and could work at a sustaining job.

Rebecca took three heavy steps into the hospital and collapsed.

Chapter 5

A yell from the other room jolted Charlie awake. The memory of the attack assailed Charlie's dazed logic. She pictured Dottie's terrified stare and rushed through the bedroom door. She swung it open and froze.

Milt sat at her table with Beth and another blonde woman across from Beth. A man sat in the fourth chair with his back to Charlie.

"Beth? What is this?" Her heart jumped into her throat, heat exploded under her skin as the adrenalin rushed through her veins. "I thought—"

Beth waved a hand and smiled. "Hey, honey, we were just playing cards. I'm sorry I got so loud, but Milton threatened to touch the deck."

"She thinks I'm bad luck for her game." Milt laughed.

Charlie inhaled to calm the race of her pulse. She dropped her shoulders and blinked away the last haze of her sleep. She noticed liquor bottles on the bar. "A party?"

"I was bored," Beth said. She gestured to the blonde woman. "I saw Lily in the hallway and Milton brought his son, Zander, to the table."

"Zander?"

The man with his back to her glanced over his shoulder.

She caught sight of his eyes and her breath lodged in her throat. Before she could say a word, he exploded out of his chair to face her.

"What in the hell happened to you?"

She stepped back. "I was attacked."

"Wait, wait, hold on here." Milt appeared between them with his arms stretched wide. "You two know each other?"

Zander said, "No."

"Yes," she said.

Realizing his answer, she raised her eyebrows and folded her arms. When she glared into those magnificent eyes, the memory of his accusations about her seeing a married man rushed forward.

"When were you assaulted?"

"What does it matter?" She held tight to her elbows otherwise she would do something she would regret later. Her heart hit fast against her bruised ribs and she swayed with dizziness.

"Easy, Ladybro." Milt reached for her elbows. "Move slow."

"What?" Zander stepped toward her again, but Milt moved between them.

"Did the medication wear off, honey?" Beth stood from the table. "I'll go get you more." Beth rushed past Zander and into the bedroom, scooping up Shadow along the way.

Charlie had forgotten about the cat in her room. Luckily, everyone focused on her. She glanced around the room as she eased onto the couch. She was grateful her injuries covered her lack of brains. "Thanks, Milt."

"Beth said you like tea. Want me to make you some?" Milt brushed his thumbs over her elbows, where he held, with concern in his eyes.

"I … I would, actually." She couldn't catch her breath. The rapid beat of her heart relentlessly pounded against her rib.

The door to her room closed. She opened her eyes to Beth's flushed face. "Here you go, honey."

Charlie lifted her eyebrows and showed her deepest gratitude for more than the Tylenol through her stare. Beth had saved her from living on the streets because Milt hadn't seen the cat. "Thank you."

"That's what I'm here for." Beth shifted back to the table.

"When were you attacked?" Zander asked.

"It happened Saturday on my run. I got involved in something I shouldn't have." She leaned back on the couch. "I'm fine."

"You call this fine?" Anger, once again, laced Zander's tone.

Milt emerged from the kitchen with a cup of tea and smacked Zander on the back of the head. "Mind your manners, boy. Charlie has been through hell. Show some respect."

"Sorry, Pop." Zander shifted to the bar, facing away.

The situation sunk in and Charlie's mouth dropped open. "Zander is Milt's son?"

"Adopted." Milt handed Charlie a cup of tea. "I love that boy."

"Love you too, Pop."

Charlie sipped the tea, mint, and smiled.

"Well, this was fun. But I've got to get to work." Lily stood. The thin blonde offered a thinner smile. Her teeth were slightly stained yellow and she gave a slim-fingered wave. The pads of her fingers looked browned. "It was nice meeting you, Charlie. Thanks for the game, Beth. Milt, Zander, I'll see you around."

Zander pivoted on his heel. "Let me walk you to your door."

"Okay." Lily glanced at Charlie before she stepped out with Zander right behind.

Charlie gingerly fingered the throb between her temples. "I didn't know you had a son, Milt."

Milt straightened the cards on the table. "He speaks before he thinks sometimes. I'm sorry about his behavior tonight. He kinda learned the overprotective stuff from me."

She nodded.

The door opened, Zander commanded the room. His stare locked on Charlie. "Was this the first time you met Lily?"

"Not tonight—er—this morning, Son." Milt answered for Charlie. "We don't want to overstay our welcome. Charlie needs her rest." Milt headed for the door. "Thanks for the game, Beth. See you ladies around."

When the door closed, Beth huffed. "You sure know how to clear a room, honey."

"Let them go," she mumbled. Released from Zander's mesmerizing stare, her lungs filled with air.

"Seems you and Zander have a connection." Beth sat at the table and fingered the stack of cards.

"Not really." Charlie had just divorced Kenneth. It wasn't right to get into another relationship so soon. She was so lost and confused about life, wanting something more, something she might never find. She couldn't start a relationship feeling half of a person.

"How do you know Zander?"

"I met him the other night when I went out." She sipped the tea. Mint and honey coated her throat, soothed her anxiety.

"The way he looks at you." Beth chuckled and shook her head. "He's too good at cards too. Beware of that one."

Charlie waved a hand and fished the coin out of her pocket. The inscription still read: BAKE TO DONATE. 5/21.

"What are you doing today?" Beth crossed her legs, yawned.

"I'm going to bake."

"Bake?" Beth laughed. "You?"

"I've got to stay focused." Charlie told Beth about the coin, how she got it, and what it instructed her to do.

"Wow, this *is* so crazy for you."

Charlie looked at her friend. "I wish I knew what this coin was trying to tell me. These bruises wouldn't hurt so bad if I knew I got them for a good reason."

Beth raised her eyebrows. "Oh?"

"Do you bake?"

"You know I don't." Beth stood and sauntered into the kitchen. "I'll tell you something else I don't do."

Charlie looked at her with silent question.

"Take out the trash." Beth held the trash bag in her hand and winked. "You need to walk around a little anyway. Work out those aches. Besides, I wouldn't know where to dump it."

"Okay, fine." Charlie stood, ignored the tightness of her muscles, and retrieved the half-full bag. "It's just in the alley. I won't be too long."

"Take your time." Beth yawned. "I'll borrow your bed for a late-morning nap."

"That's what partying all night gets you."

"Lovely." Beth headed for the bedroom, and Charlie slipped on shoes and a jacket she kept by the door.

After Charlie passed two doors in the hallway, the third swung open. Charlie's heart pounded at the sudden gust of air passing her face. She paused and tightened her grip on the trash bag.

Maria rushed from the open door, her face red and her eyes wide. A heavenly sweet scent trailed her body. When she spotted Charlie, her hands shook. "Please, please, help me."

Charlie nodded. "Yes, what?"

"Come inside." Maria disappeared into the apartment.

Charlie entered and closed the door.

Maria's apartment had a plain beige carpet the size of the living and dining room combined, and an ornate sofa that must've cost an arm and a leg by the fine quality of the dark-blue cushion covers. The carved white wood spiraled in the middle and along the legs of a two-person loveseat. She had an accent chair that matched the carpet and the sofa, completing the set. Ornate, white end tables matched the wood in the furniture.

When Maria hurried past the dining table, Charlie followed. Pink doilies spread on the white table like placemats, but Charlie couldn't imagine eating on such beauty. A vase of fresh purple flowers sat in the middle.

On the separating bar, a line of unlit candles rested on a long plate.

In the kitchen, Maria stopped before the stove. "I think I really messed these up. I need someone else to test them. I'm making cookies for the YWCA's bake sale tonight and … well … here."

Maria held out a cookie shaped like a doughnut. The chocolate frosting mimicked icing and colorful sprinkles finished the treat. Flour, dirtied mixing bowls, and a sack of salt sat on the countertops.

Charlie took the cookie and examined the palm-sized treat. "It looks good. Smells good."

"Taste it." Anxiety filled Maria's eyes. Eyes like Dottie's when she had spotted the boys in the alley.

Charlie tucked away the image. One day wasn't enough time to forget that experience. "Okay."

The cookie was rough against her lips and tongue. On first bite, her gag reflux threatened. She rushed to the sink and spit out the cookie. "Oh my gosh. That's horrible."

"Salty, right?" Maria's voice quivered.

"Yeah, it's salty." Charlie's spit more out and ran the water. She scooped water into her palm. The first drink washed away the strong flavor. The second washed away the crumbs. She turned off the water and accepted a towel from Maria.

"I was afraid I put in salt instead of sugar. I can't eat flour products, so, I didn't know how to taste it. Thanks so much for coming in. I hate the idea of salty cookies at the bake sale." Maria rubbed the back of her neck. The red in her face had lightened. She glanced around her kitchen like she was lost.

"Is everything okay?"

"I'm really behind now. They're counting on me to make these cookies and I've ruined these two batches. I'm not sure how I'm going to get it all done before nine."

"Nine?" Charlie set the towel aside, next to the dirty dishes.

"Yes, I've got to have them there by tonight. They're having a big dance. It's a great time to sell the cookies." Maria's hands shook. "Oh, dear, I guess I better get busy."

"Can I help?" The words fell out of her mouth before she thought about it.

Maria studied Charlie's features. Her tight expression relaxed. "Really?"

"I've never cooked before, but I learn fast." She lifted her free hand. "I've get a extra pair of hands to offer."

The corner of Maria's eyes wrinkled with her wide smile. "Much appreciated."

"Sure, I was just taking out the trash. I've got nothing else to do."

"Oh, mine needs to go out too. Just set yours under the sink next to mine and we can take them out later. I've got to get baking. Do you mind?"

"Not at all. Tell me what you need me to do." Charlie set the trash down, washed her hands, and accepted an apron Maria handed to her. "This'll be fun."

Marie placed a big bowl on the counter by the bar. "We'll have to triple the recipe. The baking only takes time. It's the decorating that's most of the labor."

"I have a friend staying with me. She was up all night. I'll let her sleep a little then I'll call her and ask her to help us.

"Oh, that's wonderful. We can get a good stack of baked cookies ready for the frosting before your friend comes." Marie hustled around the kitchen. "Thank you so much." The light in Maria's eyes made Charlie smile.

"No problem."

"Let's get the first batch cooking."

"Okay. What do you want me to do?"

"Measure out the sugar. The recipe is right there." She pointed at a card on the counter next to a coffee cup.

"Okay." She reached for the coffee cup and started reading the sacks for sugar. When she found it she started pouring.

"Wait," Maria interrupted. "That's a coffee cup."

Charlie raised her eyebrows. "Yes?"

Maria studied her features. "You really don't know how to cook, do you?"

A blush heated Charlie's cheeks. She shrugged.

"Here, let me help you."

The women worked companionably together for the next several minutes. Charlie couldn't believe how much sugar went into these cookies. After Maria demonstrated the teaspoon drop onto a flat pan, Charlie filled her own pan with dough balls. "Where did you learn to cook, Maria?"

"I've been cooking all my life, dear." Maria's friendly tone set Charlie at ease. "I'm surprised your mother didn't show you how to make cookies."

"My mother wasn't the baking type." Words fell out of Charlie's mouth easily. "She was more about what my father could buy her than raising a child. After my father caught her cheating on him, she left without looking back."

"I'm sorry to hear that."

"It was a long time ago, when I was ten." Charlie ignored the tightening in her chest with the memory of bags in her mother's hands. "She didn't even say goodbye."

"It's hard for a mother." Maria's voice dropped into a thoughtful tone. "It was hard for me too."

"You have children?" Surprised, Charlie stopped dropping cookies on her pan and glanced at Maria. Her gray-black hair hung in a short, loose ring of curls around her face.

"I had one." Maria's soft features hardened slightly. "I didn't do right with her."

Charlie blinked, refocused on her dough, and asked, "What do you mean?"

"I had a daughter. Her dad left me to deal with the girl. At that time, it was different, being pregnant and single. I had graduated high school but I didn't have the scores for college. I wanted to go to college. Instead, I ended up doing a lot of things to get money. Things I'm not proud of." Maria placed two pans filled with cookie dough into the preheated oven.

Charlie passed her two pans of cookie-dough balls, not as uniformed as Maria's.

Maria offered a small smile and set them on the stove. "We'll put them in next." She grabbed two glasses, poured something from the fridge into them, and handed one to Charlie.

"Thanks." The sweet lemonade cooled her from the inside out.

Maria continued, "When my daughter was in high school, she got pregnant. I guess kids follow their parents footsteps no matter how many times they're told to do things differently."

Charlie thought about her relationship with Kenneth and how it ended. He had cheated on her like her mother had cheated on her father.

"When my daughter told me about the child, I did the wrong thing. I panicked. I thought about another mouth to feed. I couldn't do it. I ended up kicking my daughter out. I told her to find a job. She had made her life difficult and I wasn't going to go through all of that again."

Maria's eyes filled with emotion. "She called me once after that telling me her boyfriend had left." Tears welled inside Maria's eyes. She shook her head. "I don't blame her for never calling back. I was mean, confused, and hurting too. But, I should've helped my daughter. I'd give anything to have another chance with her."

Charlie wiped her hands on the apron. "Maybe someday you will."

"I don't know." Maria sniffed, brushed at her eyes, and traded the cookie sheets in the oven. She slid the cooked ones onto a wire wrack before she answered, "If I did, I'd probably give her a big hug and apologize for being such a horrible mother."

Maria's pain and sadness reflected in her defeated posture. Charlie set her hand on Maria's shoulder.

"Okay." Maria gave Charlie a small roll of paper. "We've got to punch out the center of these cookies before they cool. It gives them the doughnut look."

Charlie followed Maria's direction. When their energy wilted, Charlie called Beth for backup decorating. Charlie said to Maria, "She's on her way."

"Good. Thanks for doing all of this." Maria refilled a bowl of chocolate and another one with sprinkles. "It means a lot to me to support the YWCA. They are a valuable resource for women like me."

"I'm glad to help."

Maria hustled back into the kitchen. Charlie continued decorating until Beth arrived. After introductions, Charlie shifted to the couch for a break.

She fished out the coin from her pocket. Even though she was tired, she tossed the coin in the air.

End over end, the gold sparkled within the light. It landed in her palm carrying heat to her forearm on contact. The new etched words read: TAKE TRASH OUT. 6/21.

She narrowed her eyes, read the words again, and glanced at Maria and Beth. How was the coin working like this?

Tired, she stood. "I can use some fresh air. I'll take out the trash now, Maria."

"We're almost done here. Beth said she wanted to go to the dance tonight and help sell the cookies. You can go too."

"Thanks, but I've had a long couple of days. I'll just take out the trash and head home for the evening." She tucked the coin in her pocket, shrugged on her jacket, and headed to the kitchen. She said, "See you later, Beth."

"Get some rest, honey." Beth waved.

Charlie strolled down the stairs and out the front door. Evening had darkened the sky with a low sunset. Snow crunched under her feet. She inhaled the crisp air and maneuvered through the front gate. At the alley, she dropped the trash into a commercial sized dumpster and headed back to the apartment gate.

Ears and cheeks burning from the cold, she hurried into the building. Before she climbed the steps, she dug out the coin and her phone rang. She answered.

"Hey, It's Corbin."

"Hi." A smile burst on her lips and a bubble formed inside her body, making her lighter on her feet. "How are you?"

"I was calling to ask you that question." The light tone to his voice lifted her spirit. "You okay today?"

"Sore." She leaned her back against the wall. "That's really nice of you to call me. Is that something you normally do for people you've helped or am I the lucky one?"

His deep laughter was charming. "I wanted to ask you out again. There's this anniversary party for the chief and I'd like you to be my date. What do you say?"

She didn't have to think. "Yes."

"Do you know the steakhouse in Bellevue's Convention Center?"

"I do." She couldn't stop smiling.

"I'll meet you there at five next Friday."

"Okay. See you then."

"Stay safe, Charlie." He disconnected.

Giddy, she tossed the coin in her palm on a laugh. She wasn't sure how the coin sparkled in the low light of the mudroom, but the beauty took her breath. Landing in her palm, warmth replaced the cold bite of winter in her skin and she read the etched words.

BRIGHTEN A CHILD'S DAY. 7/21.

A good night sleep appealed to her tired and sore body. She hurried to her third-floor apartment and closed the door. She flipped the light table switch and glanced around at the boxes. A wave of irritation coursed through her system.

"A movie and rest will have to wait. Time to take ownership of my life."

A heavy knock echoed off the door. She pivoted on her heel, mind absorbed by the new mess, she opened the door without glancing through the eyehole.

Zander stood tall before her.

Surprised, she stopped breathing. "Hello."

"Hi." He gestured to the toolbox in his hand. "I told Pop that I would change your showerhead."

Great, she pressed her lips. She didn't want him in her bedroom tonight when she couldn't even breathe around him. And, she wasn't sure he wouldn't tell Milt about her cat. She folded her arms. "Look. I don't mean to be rude but come back later."

She swung the door, but his boot blocked the closure.

Her heart hammered and heat exploded under her skin. She glared at him.

He shrugged his wide shoulders. "It'll just a take a couple of minutes."

She held the door tighter. "I am tired and not up for a visitor."

"I didn't want to have to do this." He waved a hand. "I know about the cat."

"Excuse me?" She stood straighter. Her heart raced for a different reason.

"I have an allergy." His half-smile was charming despite her irritation. "I discovered you had one when I walked in to play poker with Beth. Let me in now. I'll take care of the showerhead and you can keep your cat for a little while longer. Pop won't find out you've got one from me. Deal?"

"Why would you do that for me?"

"I'm one of the good guys."

Something blossomed inside her while she studied the deep bronze in his eyes. She stepped back then headed to the kitchen. "Would you like some tea?"

"I'm not a big tea drinker." He closed the door, set the toolbox down, and followed her. She looked at him studying her and heat rose in her cheeks. He casually rested a hip against the kitchen bar then folded his muscled arms over his broad chest. His suggestive smile made her stomach flutter.

He said, "But I'm up for anything."

Chapter 6

Charlie pinched her nose at the awful odor of burnt eggs. She scraped the pan into the trash. Zander entered the kitchen in the jeans and shirt he wore last night, and hugged her in his strong arms. Her frustrations of a failed attempt at cooking melted away when she lost herself into his golden-flecked brown eyes.

"Making breakfast?" His warm lips caressed her neck.

"I tried." She ran her hands along his shoulders to his hair. "Your hair is wet."

"I installed the showerhead." He kissed her cheek. "I've got to check in at work."

Her fingers enjoyed the taut skin on his muscled neck. She kissed his chin.

His smile warmed her heart. He asked, "What are you going to do today?"

"I thought I'd rest." She traced his thick, dark eyebrows with the pad of her fingers and smiled. She liked the hard edges of his face. They reflected the rest of his body. "I didn't get much last night."

He kissed her again and picked up an apple from a basket on the counter then he patted her butt then headed to the door. He gathered the toolbox. "I'll call you later, sweetheart, okay?"

"Okay." Her cheeks hurt from smiling so much. "Bye."

The door closed. Silence rang in the air. She inhaled peace and basked in the fresh memories of her pleasurable experience last night. She normally didn't go for the one-night-stand types. The way Zander held her, touched her, and took care of her, taught her something about her marriage.

Kenneth and she never had explosive chemistry.

Her phone rang. She rushed to her pants pocket in the bedroom. "Hello? Did you forget something?"

"How come I didn't see you at your desk yesterday or today?"

"Kenneth?" Her heart pumped extra blood to her body from her exertion. Her bruised rib pounded. A wave of tiredness overwhelmed her. She ran her hand along Shadow's dark fir and sat on the bed next to him.

"Damn right. Who else would I be?"

She bit her lip.

"Get your lazy ass out of bed and in the office."

His angry tone reminded her of the alley fight. Charlie had spoken up for Dottie and possibly saved Dottie from a senseless beating against the young bully.

Charlie deserved the same respect, didn't she? And this time she wouldn't get hit.

Heat surfaced in Charlie's cheeks at the thought of what she was about to do. She trembled with extra energy. She cleared her throat and found an authoritative tone. "I'm not at my desk because I quit. Remember?"

"We decided that was a mistake."

She raised her voice. "You decided it was a mistake."

Shadow ran into the other room.

"Calm down." His tone changed from argumentative to condescending.

She huffed. "I am not one of your adolescent floozies. Don't you dare use that tone with me! I demand your respect. We were married for almost two years and I did everything I could to make them good."

"Okay." He cleared his throat. "You're right, but you can't leave me here without a replacement."

She narrowed her eyes at the wall as if he were standing before her. "You're a cheating, lying, bastard and I don't want to work for you ever again. Get that through your thick skull. I quit. Done. Hire your own damn replacement. I'm sure you have a book full of numbers willing to bend over backwards for you."

"Charlie, you don't want to do this. Please. I need you." His tone dropped to a guilt-wrenching level.

"Kenneth." She fisted her hand at her side. This would be the end of his bullying. "We're done."

"You have no idea what you're talking about." He growled. "This isn't the end."

"Was that a threat?"

"Charlie—"

"No. You listen now." Anger boiled in her veins. She pointed at the wall where she imagined his ghost image. "You should have thought about how much I meant to you a long time ago before you shoved your dick in another woman. If you ever call me again, I will press charges. Do you understand?"

"Jesus, what the—?"

She disconnected before her heart exploded from the marathon running in her chest. A heavy weight lifted off her shoulders despite her rush of adrenaline. Confidence ballooned in her chest. She trembled and smiled at the same time.

"Did you just do what I think you did?"

She gasped. Beth stood in the bedroom doorway.

Charlie couldn't contain the rush. She exhaled. "Can you believe it?"

Beth smiled. "About time."

"It felt good."

"Sometimes it is good to tell someone off. Kenneth definitely deserved it."

Awed by the relief, she barely noticed Beth had changed clothes. "You look well rested for someone who was out all night."

Beth's smile widened.

She removed her robe. She wasn't shy in front of her best friend. Charlie grabbed jeans and a t-shirt. She loved listening to Beth's adventures in life and men. "How was the party?"

"Maria's cookies were the bestseller of the night and I met a really nice guy…"

Charlie's thoughts floated back to what she had just done on the phone. Before she would cower to Kenneth's bullying. Today, she didn't let him intimidate her. A warming sensation bloomed inside her chest.

She finished buttoning her jeans. She shrugged on her shirt before she looked at Beth again and realized she partially listened to Beth's story. Guilt twisted the muscles in her shoulders. "You spent the night with him?"

"We talked."

"Just talked?" Charlie raised her eyebrows. "Really?"

Beth folded her arms and nodded. "Like I said, this guy is different from the rest of the guys I've dated. We're going to see each other again next week."

Charlie brushed past Beth to start unpacking. She glanced at the door, where suitcases lined the wall. "Are you moving in with me?"

"Someone has to make sure you don't get into more trouble. Besides. I'm beginning to like it here." Beth plopped onto the couch.

"Me too." Charlie tore open the box in front of her then stopped. "I don't really want to unpack. I'm feeling good about telling Kenneth off. Kind of satisfied in a way. I want to do something else."

"What should we do?"

Charlie reached into her pocket and retrieved the golden coin.

"Oh, is that the coin you told me about?"

Charlie hadn't realized Beth was a good listener too. Maybe it was that Charlie didn't have much to say until she started flipping the coin. She nodded.

"I can't believe you actually sang in public. Didn't you have a phobia about that?"

"Yes. I'm not a very good singer, but Rebecca, the shop owner, was wonderful. She harmonized beautifully with me. It made me feel like we were connected even when I don't really know her. I actually had fun with it." Charlie turned the coin over in her hand. Her pulse calmed and her breathing eased.

Beth asked, "What was the name of the hot police officer you told me about? The one who took you to dinner after you filed charges?"

"Corbin Black. We made another date..." She stopped herself.

Zander was a player and Corbin was a keeper. Things could get complicated if she didn't do something about it. She didn't want to bring down her mood. Right now, anything seemed possible.

At Beth's unusual silence, Charlie sat beside her on the couch. Maybe Charlie had focused too much on herself. Sensitive to people who neglected good listeners, typically being the good listener, Charlie swayed her focus. "Are you okay?"

"Yeah, yeah." Beth shook her head and swallowed. "Fine. I'm fine."

Charlie looked at the coin in her palm. "The cookies we made with Maria were part of this too. I usually steer clear of someone asking for help."

"I know," Beth said. "You don't like to get tangled up in new things without some sort of background check."

Charlie giggled because it was true. "But I liked helping Maria."

Beth's eyes widened. "Really?"

"I might even volunteer for the YWCA. Someday. I didn't really know what they did before." She read the coin. "BRIGHTEN A CHILD'S DAY. What do you think that means?"

Beth took the coin from Charlie and examined the gold for a moment. She stood and held out a hand. "Come on. I've got an idea."

…

Cold air nipped at the tips of Zander's ears. He hunched deeper into his coat and hurried through the streets for his meeting with the team. Fresh air marked a new day and a new perspective on his current case. Hustling into the Puget Sound Energy building, he spotted the three guys waiting for him in the lounge.

He gestured to the restaurant counter and hurried in line. Charlie's other talent made up for her lack of skill in the kitchen. He wouldn't have pegged her as a sex goddess. Sometimes it was nice to be wrong.

He worked his way through the line ordering black coffee and a breakfast sandwich then he hustled around the corner. Early last night, Zander requested EJ get the team together so he could discuss the Dixon case.

Down the hallway, EJ had rented a conference room. Keeping the meeting locations random helped maintain cover. If anyone saw him going into the police station, he would have to explain the suspicion away. Criminals were decent at spotting lies. He didn't need the more doubt about his story while he was undercover.

Zander entered the small, windowless space and set his breakfast at a spot on the round table. EJ entered the room, glanced at everyone, and closed the door behind him. He was the Special Agent in Charge of three intelligence teams: one tactical, one investigative, and one strategic. The tactical team made arrests; the investigative team helped build cases for prosecution; and the strategic cultivated selected resources for future subversion.

Special Agent Jonah Greer worked within EJ's strategic team. He attended most of the big meetings in case they wanted to shift the investigation into a resource. Considering the amount of business the targeted meth house did, the department didn't want to overlook catching a bigger target by deeper infiltration of the house rather than busting it. If that case happened, Greer had all the Intel history he needed to continue the objective.

Agent Ellis Morgan, Agent Tyler Walters, and Agent Arnold Hunter worked on Zander's team. Two others actively monitored Lance Dixon while Zander was busy. They would get the meeting notes later.

"All right," EJ began. "What do we have, Zander?"

"I found Lance Dixon's missing sister, Lily Wallace, last night."

EJ's eyebrows rose when he sat. "We've been looking for months."

"She lives in my father's building, moved in two weeks ago. I played some poker with her yesterday and walked her to her door. She wouldn't let me in, but I called Hunter to keep an eye on her."

Zander opened the sandwich in front of him. His stomach growled with the scent of warm ham, cheese, and egg.

Hunter said, "When she left this morning, I set up surveillance equipment in her apartment. She's got boxes everywhere. I peeked in a couple and found a meth kit. She certainly uses or knows someone who does. I didn't find the actual drug anywhere in her apartment though. It's likely she'll go looking for some soon."

"Unless she's gone cold turkey like Dixon," EJ put in.

Zander hated to report the next news, but he started, "Charlie Davies lives in the same building. She was the host of our poker party."

EJ whistled, produced thick file folders to the table from his briefcase, and leaned forward on his arms. "That's a big coincidence."

Zander hated the idea of potential crime activity that could put his father out of his job and his apartment. Milt liked being the landlord. He liked being there for people. If he lost his job because his screening procedures weren't good enough for the building owner, he would have nowhere else to go.

Zander sunk the thoughts of his father into the back of his mind. Charlie's beat-up face surfaced. "Apparently, Charlie was assaulted some time in the last few nights."

"Yep." EJ slid a file towards Zander. "Ms. Charlotte Davies got into a fight with two members of the West Street gang. Mostly teenage kids involved in misdemeanor crimes. In this incident, Ms. Davies was an innocent bystander giving a cup of coffee to a homeless woman, when the group of four gang members approached. The homeless woman's name is Dottie Young. She has a son named Sage. Sage is one of the suspects of the assault. He's charged with aiding the assault. Sage has been arrested three other times for domestic assault on his mother. She never pressed charges."

"Sounds like a winning family." Zander flipped through the report. He fingered through another file on the West Street gang. Like EJ said, mostly misdemeanors, no drugs or drug distribution.

EJ continued, "There's not much in Charlotte Davies's file. No arrest record. Not even a parking ticket. I asked Hunter to expand our search and do some digging of his own on the web."

This information confirmed Zander's instincts about Charlie. She was innocent in all of this. He kept conversation light last night, wanting to earn her trust. The problem came this morning when he woke. She was something, not like the other women he played with. He found himself wishing he had met her under different circumstances. Zander's attention snapped to Hunter opposite him at the table.

Hunter said, "Ms. Davies has spent some extended time in Mexico. I'm not sure why yet."

"She recently tweeted about a rare coin. She's asking her network for information about it. I'm not sure how it applies, but she's very concentrated on the thing."

EJ asked. "Do you know anything about it, Zander?"

"No." Zander rubbed the tension building in his shoulder. He didn't find needles or a drug kit of any kind in his search of her apartment last night.

Hunter continued, "At two this morning, a large deposit was made into Davies's bank account."

"How large?" EJ asked.

"Twenty thousand dollars. I'm tracking the origin, but it's taking a while. The firewall is painstakingly involved. It's obvious, nobody wants that account found."

"Any contact with her ex-husband, yet?" EJ questioned.

Hunter shook his head. "Zander?"

"Not that I know of," he stated.

EJ leaned back in his chair. "Seems like we've got a rich kid in the mix with Dixon and Wallace. We need to understand this connection more."

Zander didn't want to let them know just how close he had gotten to her last night. He wasn't sure why; his decision went against protocol and everything he believed in, but he couldn't bring the words to his lips. His shoulder throbbed.

Zander drank his warm coffee and grimaced. "Yes, sir. Shouldn't be a problem."

EJ continued, "Hunter, keep your attention focused on Lily Wallace. I want to know if she sets up a meeting with her brother or Ms. Davies."

"Yes, sir." Hunter nodded. "I'll let you know when I break through security on the bank account. Twenty thousand dollars can buy a lot of drugs."

"Or help sustain a meth house," EJ added.

Chapter 7

Charlie unpacked the last moving box and looked at the time on her phone. Today, she had a vet appointment for Shadow. She had called and canceled on Sunday because of her pain from her injuries. The earliest the vet had was this Wednesday.

Later tonight, Zander planned to stop by.

She smiled while she checked her phone. A series of Twitter notifications from last night about the coin listed on her home screen. One of the replies had an address close to her location. She decided to stop by the Bellevue Rare Coins shop on her way to the vet's office and she needed to leave now.

Not wanting Shadow spotted by Milt, she set up a play zone in her bedroom. She couldn't bring herself to move the blanket in the corner. He seemed comfortable there, so, she left it. She put the litter box under a small desk space in the kitchen and covered it with a decorative tablecloth. If it started to stink, she could open the sliding door for air. The not-so-pleasant necessity of owning a cat.

She never thought of herself as a cat owner. Her childhood pets were more along the lines of horses. But she visited the barn; she didn't take care of the animals. The last few days, taking care of Shadow eased the ache in her chest about her empty life.

She retrieved the cat carrier she had bought yesterday while she was out with Beth. The bag looked more like a business tote than a kennel. She lifted Shadow off the couch and placed him in the new tote. "Time to go, little one."

With the coin in her pocket, the cat in the bag, and her jacket pockets holding her essentials, she grabbed the condensed boxes by the front door and headed out.

Beth left early this morning. Something to do with Maria.

Charlie hurried down the stairs without hurting her ribs and went directly into the storage area near Milt's apartment.

The storage space, organized into walled pods, was more of a large walk-in closet for the tenants. Lights were motion-activated. Her designated spot was toward the back. A chain-linked fence door could be locked for each pod, but Charlie didn't need to protect boxes from getting stolen. If someone wanted them, so be it.

Besides, she didn't think anyone could walk out of here with something and not get noticed by Milton.

She passed a strange odor and glanced at the apartment number overhead. The storage space belonged to the tenant Charlie had met on Monday, Lily. Making a mental note to tell Lily about the sour smell, she hurried to her spot in the back. She didn't have anything in her space and the boxes fit easily.

Not wanting to chance a scene with Milt, she rushed out of the apartment building and into the snow. Water puddled on the sidewalk, and dark clouds loomed above the uncrowded street. Most the cars on the road were parked. Most cities in the Seattle area didn't have a large number of snowplows. When it snowed, most people stayed home.

Over the drifts of snow and through the slow-moving city, she walked a path to the coin shop on NE Fourth Street. Nestled in a street mall, through a plowed parking lot in front, she entered.

The space was deep with rows of display cases. Inside the cases were treasures of many kinds. Stuffiness in the air made her advance with caution.

A man stood in the back corner. He had gray hair and nutmeg age spots on his pale cheeks. He looked up at her with a warm smile. "Good morning. Is there something I can help you with?"

"Yes." She marched over blue carpet and under bright lights to the counter. "I have a rare coin and I wondered if you could tell me about it."

"Sure." He held out a hand. His calm mood set her at ease. "I'm Greg Strike. You from around here?"

She introduced herself, shook his hand and fished out the coin from her pocket. "It's a magical coin."

Mr. Strike retrieved a velvet-covered tray from behind the display case and gestured for her to set down the coin. He slipped on white gloves. "You said magical?"

"See, the inscription, it changes when I flip it." She knew by the amused look on his face that she sounded crazy. She explained her experience while he studied the coin using weird looking microscopes and measuring tools.

"Yesterday, my friend and I gave out balloons to some kids at Bellevue Square. It was a fun experience for both of us. The smiles we got were awesome." It reminded Charlie that the simplest things could make a day wonderful. Spending time with her best friend was nice too. It was more fun then jet-setting like they had in the past.

Greg nodded, turned the coin in his fingers, and looked at her again. "So, have you volunteered your seat yet?"

"No. That's the next task. The eighth one." She kept her eye on the coin in his steady hands. "Can you tell me anything about the markings on the coin?"

"I haven't seen anything like this before. I could tell you a ton of things that it's not, but I'm completely stumped about where it came from or who made it." He set down his tools and looked at her with puzzlement in his deep brown eyes. "It takes a lot to confuse me when it comes to coins. I asked if you had given up your seat so I could see the coin change."

"So, you believed me when I said it was magical?"

"Why wouldn't I? You've got nothing to gain by lying to me. I will pay you for the metal in the coin, anyway."

"Oh." She frowned. "Is there anyone else who can help me identify the markings?"

"I own the store and I've been in this business for over fifteen years. However, I could take the coin and have my colleagues look at it. It's a small possibility they may know something I don't."

"Ah." She hesitated. "I don't think that's a good idea."

"Like I said before." He stood straighter, not quite her height. His dark brown stare unsettled her nerves. "I'll buy it from you based on the weight and type of metal that's in it. My scale is in the back room."

A nervous snake slithered through her body and she reached for the coin. "I just wanted to know if the coin had history or was recognizable."

"I'm sure it has history." He set his gloved hand over the coin to restrict her access. "Give me a moment to weigh it and I'll let you know how much I'll pay for it."

"No, no. Don't go through all the trouble." Her mouth dried with building apprehension. Heat coursed through her body.

"At least, let me take some photographs and I'll look into the markings for you. My camera is in the back. Just give me a moment."

She politely pushed his fingers to the side, picked up her coin, and smiled. With the coin back in her possession the tension in her body ebbed. "It's not for sale."

His gloved fingers gripped her wrist in a loose hold. "Have you thought the coin might be leading you on a wild-goose chase? What if the things you are doing are going to make your life harder?"

She yanked her wrist free. "I don't know what you're talking about."

He leaned forward. "I'm a old man and I listen well, my dear. I heard it in the story you didn't tell me, the tone of your voice, and your body language. You're doing the things the coin tells you because you're searching for something. Am I right?"

His uncanny observation disturbed her. She didn't reply.

"We're all searching for something." His smile wasn't as warm as when she first walked into the store. "I'll be happy to take the coin from you. It's a fascinating mystery and you'll make money on the deal. Don't you need money?"

"I said no, thanks." She eased toward the front of the store.

He waved, his smile pasted on his face, his eyes glued to her body. "I'll be here if you change your mind."

Outside the building, Charlie realized her phone was vibrating in her pocket and she answered.

"Hey, sweetheart." Her father's calm voice caressed her eardrums.

She hurried across the street. "Hey, Dad. What are you up too?"

She didn't hear his reply. Mr. Strike exited his store and stood on the front walk with his arms folded against the cold. He stared at her as she rushed around a corner, behind the cover of a city building. Her heart raced.

"Sweetheart, are you okay?" Her father's worried tone brought her mind back to the conversation.

"Yeah, ah, yeah." She ignored the ache in her ribs from her exertion and slowed her pace now that she couldn't see Mr. Strike or the coin store. "Yeah, I'm okay. What's going on, Dad?"

"I just wanted to"—he cleared his throat—"I mean, you know, I'm here for you, right? If you need anything. If you're in trouble."

She rushed down 110th Street, past strangers in thick coats. Traffic had picked up since she had entered the store, but moved slowly in the slick snow. "Yeah, Dad, I know. We've got each other, right?"

"Right." His silence was unusual.

Charlie stopped walking. "What is it?"

"I just wanted to make sure you were okay." His voice cracked. "I look forward to visiting in a few days."

"Me too." She inhaled the cold air, glanced around at nothing.

"Well, okay, talk to you this weekend." He said.

She narrowed her eyes. "You really okay, Dad?"

"Yeah, yeah, talk to you later sweetheart."

"Okay, bye," she disconnected. Something was up. She figured she'd find out this weekend. Right now, she had to get to the vet.

…

Rebecca sat on the edge of her bed, with her hands cradling her wet face. Tears streamed down her cheeks. She couldn't tell Decker about closing the store at the same time they found out she was pregnant.

Decker was thrilled about the child. His deep-rooted joy filled her heart. Her big man had a new future, a new purpose. Three long months of sitting next to his bed, encouraging him when she was doubtful herself. And the news of the baby did the trick. He wanted to be out of the hospital as soon as possible.

The doctors said he could leave the hospital in a few weeks.

Unfortunately, the damage to his back wasn't completely healed and he couldn't work right away. He needed to start small, learn to use a cane every day. He said that wasn't an issue because they owned the store and he could set his recovery pace. He would be ready to hold the baby when the time came.

Rebecca wailed in the darkness of the room.

She left the hospital tired, her stretched emotions torn. Two mouths to feed were enough stress. Now there was a third. A child.

Her hopes of Decker supporting the family while she raised the children and ran the community store were crushed. The firefighting accident had rendered him physically disabled for life.

The studio apartment above her closed shop wasn't big enough for a family. Her chances of finding a job were lower than before. Who would hire a pregnant woman?

...

After the vet appointment, Charlie maneuvered through the unusually tight crowd on the bus. When she found a handhold, the bus jerked into motion and she asked a stranger, "What's going on in Bellevue today?"

"Live music in the park. It'll be going on till next Monday."

The bus juddered to a stop and the stranger exited. Charlie slid into a vacated seat, thankful for the reprieve. Shadow wasn't a big cat to lug around, but she wasn't used to the work. Her bruised ribs ached and she was ready for a nice cup of tea.

A dark-haired man escorted a short pregnant woman onto the bus. The couple looked around for a seat when the bus jerked into motion. Without a word, Charlie remembered the coin toss and offered her seat to the couple by gesturing.

The man smiled his thanks and the woman dropped into the chair, exhaling.

Charlie propped herself against a handrail beside the door. Her knees ached from her exercise today. Tiredness crept into her other muscles. The bus stopped at her corner and she hurried off.

She took the route slow, careful with her footsteps, trying not to jar her ribs anymore. The cold air pinched her cheeks. Clear skies teased of better weather ahead. Her mind wondered to the coin and she fished it out of her pocket.

Her thumb rubbed over the smoothed surfaces of the coin, and she tossed it into the air. It flipped end over end, flashing like a polished diamond in the sky. Enchanted, her breath caught in her throat. The coin landed into her palm. Its weight balanced her somehow.

Fascinated by the warmth cascading up her forearm, she opened her palm. She read: WRITE A LETTER OF RECOMMENDATION. 9/21

She pocketed the coin, turned into the gate to her apartment, and climbed the stairs. She was eager to move forward with her coin toss. While she maneuvered around her apartment feeding the cat and making tea, she wondered for whom she would write a letter of recommendation.

She glanced around her apartment and smiled, then retrieved her nicest letterhead with an envelope. It didn't take her long to write the letter. She rushed out of her apartment, down the stairs, and knocked on Milton's door.

This was the right thing to do at the moment. She needed to find enrichment in her life. She wanted to make a difference, somewhere.

When he didn't answer, she slid the letter under the door and fished out the coin from her pocket. She tossed it. The gold lit up the dimly lit room as it turned end over end. Taking its time. It landed in her palm warm to the touch.

VOLUNTEER FOR A TASK 10/21

At the top landing she ran into Lily, the new tenant. "Hi."

"Hi, Charlie, right?" Lily's slim body shook under her thick coat.

"Yeah." Charlie's concern spiked. "Are you okay?"

Lily's blonde eyebrows drew together in silent question. "You're shivering."

"Oh, ah, I've got a fever." Her thin voice wobbled. "I'm off to see my, ah, doctor about it."

"Well, stay warm." Charlie stepped to the side. "They say the sun won't last to tomorrow."

"Thank you." Lily paused two feet in front of her. The woman needed a breath mint. She held a package in her bony hands. "I'm not sure how long this visit is going to take. I talked with my doctor on the phone and I think he might want me to stay the night for, ah, observation. But I promised a friend I would deliver this package. You run in the morning, don't you? Beth said something about that the other night."

"Yeah." Charlie's intuition reared in the back of her mind. "I run every morning."

Lily rattled off an address. "You pass there?"

Charlie nodded.

"Would you mind running this errand for me? I would owe you big time."

Charlie wasn't sure she wanted to involve herself in Lily's affairs. Her fingers stroked the coin in her pocket and she nodded despite her instincts. "Okay."

Lily handed the package to Charlie. "I owe you one. Thanks so much."

"Sure."

Lily hurried down the stairs and Charlie realized she had forgotten to mention the smell in the storage room surrounding Lily's things. After she delivered the package tomorrow, she would stop by Lily's.

Satisfied that her errand was in play via package in the morning, Charlie hustled to her apartment. She closed the door, flipped the light table switch, and let Shadow out to play. The cat tore off into the bedroom.

Charlie strolled into the kitchen for some tea. She withdrew the cup from the corner store, but switched it. She had a good day.

She put the kettle on and put the certificate from the vet visit on the refrigerator. The adoption was complete. Shadow was her responsibility. When she got time and a little spending cash, she would buy a frame for the document.

She opened a can of food, spread it out on a plate, and called Shadow to dinner.

She washed the pear from the fridge, took a bite, and considered Shadow while he ate. New warmth nestled inside her. Pride? Maybe. Caring? More likely. Whatever it was, it added a bucket of water to the empty pool in her soul.

Shadow needed her and she found comfort with him.

Her mind drifted to Zander. She withdrew the phone from her pocket. Someone had called and left voice mail earlier.

"This is Greg Strike from Bellevue Rare Coins, you met me this morning."

Charlie's eyebrows rose along with her tension. Where did he get her number?

"I've been looking into the markings on your coin. I think I have something that would interest you. Please call me back." He recited a phone number.

A knock at the door jolted her concentration.

…

Zander had called Dixon earlier today. No luck getting together. The man was buttoned up tight.

Charlie opened the door. She shifted from one foot to the other. The black eye didn't distract from her natural beauty. If she wore make-up, he couldn't tell. Rose color in her pale cheeks reminded him of brushed satin sheets. Her long lashes framed inquisitive, unforgettable green eyes.

Maybe he was foolish in thinking she wasn't involved in drugs. She was clever enough to sponsor a meth house without anyone asking questions.

"Hi, you're beautiful." Earning her trust was his next big objective.

"Hi. I was just thinking about you."

"Were you?" He entered the room, brushed a kiss on her neck, and smiled. "Missed me?"

"Just thinking about you." She closed the door. "What have you got there?"

He lifted the bags he carried. "Dinner. Hope you don't mind. I picked up a rotisserie chicken, some steamed veggies, and some fresh bread."

"Why would I mind?" Her wide smile was warm.

He had read her profile. What would she tell him about herself that he didn't already know? He walked into the kitchen and started unpacking the bags. "You mentioned before that you had traveled with Beth. Where is your favorite place?"

The kettle whistled. Her hands shook when she poured the water. "I suppose Mexico is my favorite. I spent a year down there with my ex-husband."

"You were married?" He played his part.

"For a year and a half. Monday, our papers were official."

He grabbed plates from the overhead cabinet then started serving the plates with hot food. His stomach rumbled and his mouth watered. "Why did you get a divorce?"

"He cheated on me." Her voice wobbled. Tension grew in her expression.

He didn't want to make her more uncomfortable, but he wanted to know more. "Did you like Mexico? What did you do there?"

"Mostly explored. Kenneth worked a lot. He makes fireworks. He's one of the best in the business. He has a production branch down there."

Zander lifted the plates and headed to the table.

Charlie grabbed some silverware, a roll of paper towels, and followed him. She sat next to him at the four-person table.

"What about you?" She ate bites of chicken. "Ever marry?"

"No. I travel a lot with my job."

"What do you do?" She looked at him with her head tilted, like a shy little girl coaxing answers out of someone who didn't want to talk. She was very astute.

"I help businesses with their future."

She folded her arms under two handful-sized breasts. The hem of her turtle-necked, long sleeve shirt ended at an average waist and flared hips. She wore something on her skin. A subtle perfume he couldn't name.

He lowered his voice. "Where did you go to college?"

"Listen, Zander." Her whisper was laced with control. She dropped her hands to the table and her eyes stared at her food. "I've been thinking about us."

He didn't like her train of thought. He laid his open palm on her hand. "What is it, sweetheart? Are you happy? I am."

Puzzled frustration filled her voice. "I'm just not sure that I can offer a relationship. I just got out of one, a bad one and—"

He leaned forward and brushed his lips against the throbbing vein in her neck.

"I don't even know you." Her voice was barely audible. She inhaled.

His body hardened, ready for whatever came next. The soft texture of her skin glided along his tongue like sweet candy. He kissed her earlobe, then nibbled there. "Maybe we just enjoy the pleasure without complications for now."

Her hands fisted on the table and she leaned closer to him.

It was hard not to rush her into doing what he wanted. He whispered, "I need to feel you under me. I've never experienced this strong of an attraction to one woman before. Why you, sweetheart? Why you?"

He caressed her arms, shifted his open hands into her shoulders and rested his spread-out fingertips closer to the hills of her breasts.

"Is it hot in here?"

"I don't think you need that sweater." He caressed his hands down the front curves of her body and hooked his fingers on her shirt.

If she wasn't a drug dealer, he was in over his head because he did want her, desperately. His hands shook with the thought. He should stop this now. All he needed from her was information and he could get that through interviewing her, he didn't have to—

She sunk her fingers into his hair, under the collar of his shirt, and whispered, "Zander, this is crazy."

"I like the way you say my name." And he did. "I like the way you taste on my tongue. I want more, Charlie. Will you give me more?"

"I'm not this kind of woman." She didn't sound upset.

"What kind of woman?" He brushed kisses along her cheek. She turned her face to him. When he reached her lips, she shifted into his arms and straddled his lap. Her long legs hugged his waist tight. Her chest melted against him, so soft and pliable.

Then, she devoured his lips in a toe-tingling, mind-blowing kiss that would have knocked him down if he weren't sitting already. Her hands explored the muscles in his arms and she rubbed the soreness in his shoulder. He groaned with the massage, the taste of her on his tongue. Innocence infused with trust emanated from her body heat.

Something deep inside of him grew while his hands skimmed down to the curve of her perfect ass. He couldn't get enough of her.

"Zander." A desperate demand filled her tone.

He yanked her closer to him, where he wanted her the most. Another moan escaped his throat with the contact. His heart raced. The boom of his attraction clouded everything else.

Heat exploded in his body from the pit of his stomach.

The door rattled.

She tore her lips away from him and looked at who came in.

He didn't care. He was making progress.

"Oh," a woman's surprise stiffened Charlie's body against him.

He glanced at Beth in the doorway.

Charlie inched away.

He didn't let her go.

"Hey, Beth." Her voice was breathy but back in control. She nudged his chest. When he didn't move, she looked into his eyes. "It's Beth."

"Hi, Beth." He let the disappointment taint his tone and locked Charlie's attention on his unwavering stare. "You've got terrible timing."

"Story of my life." Beth stepped into the apartment, not out.

Zander exhaled and conceded his tight hold on Charlie.

She blinked out the rest of his hard work in getting her to relax in his arms and stood. She adjusted her clothes and cleared her throat. "We were just having dinner."

"Oh, good, I'm starved." Beth shrugged out of her jacket and hurried to the table. "What are we eating?"

Chapter 8

Zander knocked on Charlie's door again. He knew she was in there. His heart pounded in his chest and the anger grew inside him like a lion out of a cage. "Open up. Why are you avoiding me?"

Elbow to the door, he forced his way inside. Two steps in, he found the place a mess. Her new television was in pieces on the floor. The material on the sofa was grated. Clothes and other items were scattered.

Sweat formed on his brow. He couldn't catch his breath. He called out to her while he hustled over the clutter.

She didn't answer.

The stench of blood made him run faster to the bedroom. There he saw her on the bed, lifeless, blood soaking the sheets. Shreds of her beautiful hair were strewn throughout the room.

Tears surfaced in his eyes. He hurried to her side and hugged her limp body. Pain shocked through his veins from his heart. He yelled out, "No. No—"

Jerking awake, Zander sat straight up in his bed. His heartbeat echoed in his ears. He blinked and focused on the things around him. He concentrated on the duffel bag in the corner. Gulping for air, he wiped away the sweat on his stubbled face.

Confused, adrenaline-filled, he kicked his legs over the edge of the couch and inhaled. He rubbed his face again while swearing at the dream. "It wasn't her. It wasn't her. It was a dream."

He had found his mother, dead, on the bed when he was thirteen. He hadn't thought about it in years. The idea of Charlie dead had him on edge. Messing around in Dixon and Wallace's business, she would be.

Personal feelings poisoned his situation. He didn't want his emotions involved. Undercover, he didn't want to care. Just do the job.

"Too late." He focused on deep breaths and cradled his face with shaking hands, elbows rested on his knees. He resisted the urge to call her and find out if she was okay. Something deep inside of him nested uncomfortably. "Fuck!"

He hurried into the bathroom and doused his heated face in cold water. The temperature shocked him the rest of the way

"The Chief's anniversary party is tomorrow." EJ coughed. "You might want to use your shopping trip to get closer to Davies today."

"Good idea, sir."

"Get to work, Agent." EJ disconnected.

Zander threw the phone to the floor and yelled. Charlie had played him in the worst way. He didn't see the siren beneath the innocence. He smashed his fists on the table, inhaled, and sat in the silence for a moment.

More in control, he retrieved the phone and dialed a familiar number. "Hey, Pop. I'm on my way over."

"Don't take too long, Son." The relief in Milt's tone burned Zander raw.

He slammed the mental door on his personal torment, grabbed a pile of clothes and headed to the bathroom for his shower. "I won't."

In record time, Zander was out the door.

Sun melted the slush under his feet. Blue skies indicated winter weather was moving on, unlike him.

City traffic had picked up on Fourth Street. He coughed through pockets of smog and rushed around the last corner, his breath heavy.

Two police cars were parked on the street. He spotted Beth coming out of the front gate. "Hey, Beth."

She paused with a shorter dark-haired woman beside her. "Zander, you know Maria?"

"Nice to meet you. Where you headed?" Zander asked Beth.

"They found my daughter," Maria said. Her far away gaze was filled with concern and tears. She held a partially used tissue in her hand. "I can't believe they called me. It's a miracle."

"A attorney called Maria this morning saying that her daughter was in a state institution and someone was pressing charges against her grandson." Beth shifted past Zander. "I'm going to help her figure it all out."

Zander didn't really care. He needed to get inside and find the package.

Beth took a couple steps away. "Excuse us."

"Is Charlie home?" He liked and hated the ease of her name off his tongue.

Beth said over her shoulder, "Charlie packed a bag and was gone before I got up."

Zander's rapid heartbeat revived when he remembered the scattered luggage in her apartment last night. "Any idea where can I find her?"

"No." Beth hugged Maria with one arm and continued on her way.

"Shit." He hurried inside the building, entered Milt's apartment without knocking, and called "Pop?" Then headed to the master-key lockbox. "Heard you had a busy morning."

Milt's main area was bigger than the tenants because the landlord suite stretched across half the bottom level. He kept things clean, tight, and in their place due to his military background. Three bedrooms and enough space in the main area for a small gym; the gym was separated from the living area by a partial wall.

The lockbox was in Milt's room under his bed.

Zander hurried through and dropped to his knees beside the bed. He fished the box out and started entering the passcode.

"Hey, boy, I gave you the passcode in case of a emergency." Milt stood in the doorway, frowning.

"I know Pop." Zander opened the box, grabbed the keys. "This is a emergency."

"For who?" Milt followed him through the apartment. "Slow down, son."

Zander raced out the door and ran up the stairs. Anxiety coiled with his stomach. He didn't want to find the package in her apartment. Irritation boiled in his veins. He shouldn't care about what he found in her apartment. It shouldn't matter.

"Just do the fucking job," he ordered himself and pressed his lips.

At her door, he sorted through the keys. His hands shook and he fought against his own body to match metal with metal.

Milt caught up to him. "What's going on?"

Zander couldn't speak. He shoved open the door and stopped when he spotted a package on the table. "Fuck."

Milt closed the door then stood beside Zander. "What is it?"

A bombshell exploded in his chest, took his breath. He inched farther inside, picked up the package, and whispered, "Please, no."

The package was a lead weight in his hands. He peeled open the paper and every muscle in his body tensed. He exhaled, long and suffering, then closed his eyes. Reality spread from his chest to the rest of his body. Dizzy. His knees threatened to buckle. He eased onto the couch. Sweat formed on his brow and his throat swelled.

Milt whistled. "That's one nice-looking necklace."

"It's stolen." Zander inhaled. "And this is cocaine packed around it."

"What does it mean?"

"I found concrete evidence." Zander shook his head and looked at his Pop. "Charlie is involved in Lily Wallace's business."

"No." Milt stepped back. "There's no way."

"I didn't want to believe it either." Zander blinked out the burn in his eyes. "God, I liked that woman too much."

"There's got to be something wrong. A logical explanation."

"Pop," Zander's voice cracked. He held the package out. "I thought the same thing, but here's the evidence."

A cat jumped onto the couch and Milt swore. "She's got a cat?"

"It's named Shadow."

"You knew about this?" Milt looked at him with accusation in his eyes.

Zander nodded. "I've got to call this in."

"Okay." Milt picked up the cat. "Sure is cute."

…

Charlie opened her eyes and smiled over the best night's sleep she had in days. At three o'clock this morning, she realized Beth slept differently as an adult. No way could they sleep in the same bed.

She stretched, an easy extension of her well-rested body, and exhaled. She climbed out of the softest sheets and blankets in the world and stood on plush evergreen carpet in her father's guesthouse.

The room's walls were light teal with white wainscoting on the bottom half. Copies of professional artwork hung on the walls in ornate frames. The four-poster bed had power white sheers draped from top to bottom and the large space held a pleasant citrus air freshener.

It was funny, her appreciation for the luxury.

She had stayed in this guesthouse many times before, thinking she was roughing it like camping. She laughed and twirled with her arms stretched wide.

She entered the bathroom. Marble countertops with golden flecks held a large sink. When she turned the knobs, water cascaded from the wide spout. She splashed the warmth on her face and neck. The silk pajamas were courtesy of her father's hospitality.

Charlie filled the oversized Jacuzzi tub with water and climbed inside. She enjoyed the blue-sky view through the skylight. She wanted this day of pampering. She needed it.

Chapter 9

Mercer Island was a wonderful, small island in the center of Lake Washington. The community was tight and limited to people who could afford premium real estate.

Charlie stood before the floor-to-ceiling windows.

The lake water sparkled. In the distance, the city stood taller than the residential neighborhoods. She opened a small refrigerator packed with fresh fruit and cheese. Her father had a concierge available, but she didn't need to bother him. She had enough to keep her happy. She had enjoyed her day yesterday. The rest helped heal the last aches and pains from the attack in the alley.

Tonight, she had a date with Corbin. They were going to a nice dinner and a party for the chief of police. Corbin mentioned the attire was semi-formal.

Her bare feet sunk into the carpet when she strolled to the walk-in closet. In the back corner was a secret door to her things. Her second favorite shoes lined the top shelf inside. She laughed at her overindulgence. She hadn't realized how much she actually spent on stuff she didn't need.

Her dresses were sorted by color. She searched through the hangers of royal purple and found the halter dress with a short hem. The lovely, form-fitting gown was her favorite girls night outfit. She grabbed a pair of silver shoes and a small Kate Spade handbag.

She had a cosmetic set hidden in the bottom drawer of the bathroom vanity. The bruise on her face had faded and she covered it well. She brushed on mascara then paused in mid-application, thinking of Zander.

Dating the men who were the opposite of her father was intentional. These men would come home for dinner every night, watch television with her, and share in her daily stories.

She grew up with her father's unreliability. There were fun times. Spontaneity had its benefits. But she hated the stretched out times she had spent alone. Weeks, sometimes months, she had gone without seeing her father. It was lonely.

Kenneth had been one of those men too, the kind who traveled.

Zander had said he traveled for work.

She frowned at herself in the mirror. Her shoulders slumped. She didn't want to be lonely or dependent anymore. Not again. Tears burned in her eyes. Her heart squeezed painfully.

The next time she saw him, she needed to keep a level head and say goodbye. She had to break things off with Zander. She deserved more.

Her phone rang. She rushed to her phone and connected. "Hi."

"Hi, Charlie." Beth's voice brought a small smile to her lips. "Where are you?"

"I'm staying at one of my father's guesthouses. I'm headed to dinner with Corbin tonight. What about you?"

"Do you have time to meet with me before your date?"

"Why?"

"Well, I wanted to talk with you in person."

Charlie looked at the clock on the wall. "I'm on Mercer Island."

"Damn." Frustration sounded in Beth's voice. "That's pretty far from me right now. 'Bout a hour and a half."

"Okay." Charlie frowned. She sat on the bed. "Well, what is it?"

"Did Maria tell you about her daughter?"

"Yeah." Charlie dropped back onto the bed and exhaled. "My heart breaks for her. She's got so much guilt about what happened."

"So you know, then. That makes this easier."

Charlie closed her eyes and asked, "Makes what easier?"

"The attack in the alley. Those boys that you're pressing charges against." Beth inhaled. "The state found the closest relative on file. Dottie is Maria's daughter and one of the boys, Sage, is Maria's grandson. They called her when the charges were going through process. Can you believe it?"

"Are you kidding?" Charlie's heart shifted into high gear. She squeezed her eyes tighter. "They're all related?"

"Yeah." Beth continued. "Maria is terrified. She just found them again and doesn't want to lose them. Dottie is facing life in a medical facility and Sage is being tried for assault. He might get time in prison. "

Charlie didn't know what to say. The doorbell buzzed. Charlie hurried to press the reply button next to the bed. "Be right down."

"What?" Beth asked.

"My driver is here." Charlie rubbed her forehead, careful of her bruised eye.

"Charlie, Maria wants to do right this time. I think she deserves another chance. I want you to think about dropping the charges."

Charlie paced the floor. "I understand what you're saying, but I'm not sure what to do. I'm not even sure if I can."

"You pressed charges before you knew the connection. Now you know, please, consider Maria. This is a big deal for her. How would you feel if they were taken away from her again?" Beth emphasized again.

Charlie glanced at the clock.

"I know you. You'd never forgive yourself." Beth continued.

"I've got to go. I'll call you later, okay?"

"Okay. Think about it."

Minutes later, she was at Bellevue Convention Center. She hurried out of the car and through the lobby to the elevators. On the way she passed an interesting glassworks shop.

She approached the hostess and followed the younger woman weaving through tables lined on the outside of the building by the windows. Charlie saw Corbin at the table.

"Hi. Let me help you with your coat." The coat slipped from her bare shoulders, and she turned back in time to see Corbin's gaze had drifted over her body. Gooseflesh formed on her skin. "You look beautiful tonight."

She slid into the tall backed booth. "Thank you. You look very nice too."

"Thanks." He settled in opposite her.

A waitress approached. She wore her long dark hair in a ponytail, a white shirt with a black tie, and a black apron matching black slacks. "Hello, welcome to David's Broiler. My name is Lauren. May I get you something to drink?"

"Just water for now, thank you." She noticed Corbin had red wine and a water glass in front of him.

"I'll be back in a moment with some bread too." Lauren hurried off.

"I was just checking my messages. I went to a bake sale the other night and met some interesting…" Corbin's voice faded to her overpowering thoughts.

Charlie looked at a tabletop candle. She didn't like what Beth proposed about the boys in the alley. She couldn't stand the idea of them getting out and hurting Dottie again. But Charlie wasn't sure she could put Maria through the torment, either.

The waitress appeared with water and a basket of bread. Warm, sweet sourdough floated into Charlie's nostrils, bringing her mind back to the table. She looked at Corbin's concerned stare and heat splashed over her cheeks.

The waitress said, "I'll be back in a minute to take your orders."

"Thanks," Corbin said.

Lauren smiled then rushed off again.

"So." Corbin opened the breadbasket, grabbed a slice, and spread butter on a piece. He offered it to Charlie, who accepted. "What's on your mind?"

She smiled. "I'm sorry. I'm just…"

He shrugged.

Charlie exhaled. "I got a call from my best friend, Beth."

"Beth?" His eyes narrowed. "Did you say Beth?"

"Yes." Charlie waved a hand at the insignificant point. "Anyway, she's become close with a neighbor of mine."

Charlie explained Beth's call. "I'm not sure what to do now."

Corbin nodded, looked around, and adjusted the collar on his mocha shirt. There was something in his eyes, something uneasy.

"You probably don't want to talk about this on your night off."

"No. It's okay." He cleared his throat. "Um … Charlie, do you bake?"

Charlie's eyebrows dropped at the change in conversation. "No. Why?"

"Err … never mind. It isn't serious right now." He exhaled.

The waitress approached the table again and took their orders.

He sipped his wine, blinked, and looked at Charlie again. "I'd like to point out a few things about your situation. I'm not advocating for one thing or the other, I just want to make sure you understand it all."

"Okay." Charlie nodded.

"I work the area every day," Corbin said. "I know Dottie and Sage by name. They live in a low-income apartment and he pays for the rent because she can't hold a job. He figures, if he pays then he can do whatever he wants to her. She never presses charges. Dottie is emotionally challenged and she can't teach him any differently."

He sat back in the booth, his hazel eyes thoughtful. "Sage is in and out of juvie. He's never there long enough to make a connection with the youth counselor. The counselor knows how to help this kid, just needs the time. Your charges will give him that time.

"And if Dottie gets the right medical attention from a professional institution, she might be able to move forward and become more self-sufficient. You could do that for her through this situation." He shrugged. "Overall, in my opinion, it the best thing that ever happened to them. They won't get the help on their own."

"I see your point." Charlie leaned back as glasses of wine arrived. Her anxiety eased, even though she still wasn't sure what to do. "Thank you."

"Another thing," Corbin continued. "This is a pattern for Sage. While he's in the system, people like you are safer on the streets."

She nodded.

He casually waved an open hand. "Besides, it sounds like proceedings are in motion. It's not likely you'll be able to drop the charges."

Charlie thought for a moment. "But, Maria."

"She'll know where they are from here on, if she wants. The choice is hers. What she does is out of your control." His attention drifted to over her shoulder.

A group of men approached a joined set of tables beside them. Past the tables was a clear view of beautiful Lake Washington in the distance. The men in the group settled and Charlie winced at the raised level of deep voices. She looked at Corbin's frown. He noticed her attention and smiled, not quite as happy as he was a few moments ago.

"From or d... the... other...."

Charlie shook her head. "I can't hear you."

He leaned in closer. "From our date the other night, I got to thinking about my brothers again." He raised his voice slightly. "I put in another search for Alexander and Decker. I haven't gotten anything back yet, but it's been a while since I first searched."

"That will be neat when you find them. What are you planning to do?" Charlie sipped the wine.

"It's been a while—"

The group's male laughter overshadowed the conversation.

Their steaks and potatoes arrived, and they enjoyed their food for the next several minutes.

"How is your coin flipping going?" Corbin's question surprised her.

"Oh no!" Her body heated with a blush. "I forgot all about the package."

"Package?" Corbin ate another bite of steak.

She was too hungry to give into the stress about her absentmindedness. Her next bite of meat fell shorter on flavor, but was still a welcomed treat. She swallowed. "I'm suppose to do an errand for someone else. I got a package from a neighbor. She wanted me to deliver it yesterday morning. I forgot."

"Deliver it later."

"She said it needed to be there this morning." Charlie's heart thumped against her chest. "What if the magic stops working because I missed a task?"

Corbin whipped out his phone. "I have a list of things to do. I'd be really happy if you helped me with a few of them."

Charlie finished the baked potato and sipped her wine. "When I flip it, the path is clear. I'm not sure how it does it. I should have delivered that package."

After she said the words, she worried about her initial reaction to Lily's request. Everything had felt right about the other tasks.

Corbin shrugged, unworried. "Maybe something else will come up. There's got to be more than one option, right? You have the choice to do the task in the first place. It makes sense that you have choices on how they are done too." He drank the rest of his wine.

"I'm not sure." She finished her meal. Charlie's mind wondered back to Maria.

Charlie asked Corbin, "If you had a wish, what would you wish for?"

He rested his hands on his lap. "To find my brothers."

She nodded in understanding.

He gestured. "What about you?"

"I was thinking about a nice home in the suburbs with a couple of kids and dinner on the table by six." she admitted.

"Dinner by six?" He laughed. "I don't get off work until eleven, tops. That's a good day. I'd probably go stir-crazy anyway. I've got to have people to talk with, about, and listen too. I'll probably own a bar or something when I retire."

...

Zander entered the grand conference hall of the Hyatt Regency hotel. The Chief's party was already underway with people going in and out of the designated room. Beige columns lined the hallway on his right, ornate brown carpet lined the floor, and square chandeliers gave off an ochre glow from the ceiling. To his left was a sculpture of twisted roots, maybe. He didn't understand modern art.

He entered the doorway to a large crowd. All the men were in slacks and button-down shirts; all the women were in fancy dresses. A live band played on a stage against the far wall. People closest to him milled around a spread of food. Waiters and waitresses, in all black, moved about.

Zander inhaled the spicy aromas, spotted EJ in the crowd, and approached with a smile. They had figured the uniforms scared Charlie off, but they also figured she would return for her things and her cat soon.

They had repackaged the items with a tracking beacon. EJ didn't tell the FBI about the find yet. They wanted a little more information before they busted the only lead they had to the meth lab.

Zander had orders to resume his cover when she returned—like nothing happened. Yeah, like he could forget the lies or that his heart broke into tiny pieces at the site of the package. He shook the thoughts from his mind and held out a hand. "Hey, EJ."

EJ took it. He cleaned up well and wore his dress clothes comfortably. He turned to his wife. "Patricia, you remember Zander?"

"Oh, yes." She held out a well-manicured hand. She had deep blue eyes that sparkled when she smiled. Her handshake was delicate in his big hands. "Good to see you again. You look great tonight, minus the dark circles that match my husband's."

Zander had worked extra hours with his Pop in effort to get the apartment building cleaned up. But Milt might lose his job after all.

"Darling." EJ's soft tone held a sliver of grit. "We're not talking about work tonight."

She returned her attention to Zander. "What do you do outside of work?"

"I read." Zander rubbed the ache in his shoulder. He glanced around the room noting Hunter at the food table then looked back at Patricia.

"I didn't figure you for the quiet type."

Extensive travel had plenty of downtime, and Zander enjoyed reading current affairs and science fiction.

"I don't suppose you read romance?" Her light pink lips framed straight white teeth.

"No, ma'am. I read one once and was bored to tears." That wasn't the complete truth. He didn't mind romance novels as long as the woman didn't give up her life for the man. He liked women who were strong enough to partner, not change into a chameleon. "Excuse me, I see Hunter and need to talk with him."

"Have a good time, Zander." EJ escorted his wife to the dance floor.

Zander found a wall to hold up. Man, he was tired. If he had one wish in his pocket, right now, it would be for a comfy meal with a woman he loved. His chest squeezed tight as he fantasized about Charlie in an apron. He shook the image away.

So many things were wrong with that thought.

He glanced around the room. The gift table was next to the stage. He had forgotten a gift. He looked at his watch figuring the time. If he ran quickly—

"Zander, what are you doing here?" He looked at Charlie.

The halter dress hugged her curves and left him with lustful thoughts. All that exposed ivory skin for licking. Not to mention the sweet aroma of her perfume. It surrounded him, punched his temptation.

He wanted to grab her, kidnap her into a quiet room somewhere, and yelled at her for lying to him. At the same time, he wanted to sweep her off her feet and make her feel half the amount of heat she gave him. He wouldn't have a job for long if he did those things. He needed to play this cool.

He cleared his throat. "You look breathtaking tonight, Charlie."

"Thanks." Rose powdered her cheeks with his compliment. She was good at pumping up his dominant character with her innocent act. "You didn't bring one, did you?"

"Bring what?" He couldn't take his eyes off the low drop of her dress, the soft curves of her breasts. "What are you talking about?"

"A gift." Her lowered tone brought his attention back to her perfectly painted lips. "You didn't bring an anniversary gift, did you?"

"Uh, no," he admitted.

"I thought so."

He did something right, he was on her mind. He smiled at the haughtiness in her voice. "How often do you think about me?"

She blinked, then glanced around. "Have you seen my date?"

The idea of her in another man's arms stabbed at his tight control. He stepped closer to her, commanding her attention. "Who?"

"Never mind. Wait here."

Her grabbed her arm. "Where are you going?"

"I'll be back." Her intelligent eyes searched his features. "What?"

He studied her puzzled expression while he mentally debated if she would return. Did she know about Lily's bust? By instinct he would say no, unfortunately, he couldn't count on instinct with this woman. "I'm not sure that I want to let you go. I missed you."

Her face glowed when she smiled. "I promise I'll be back and we can dance together. Okay?"

"What about your date?"

She waved a hand. "He's busy mingling with all his friends anyway."

Zander couldn't hold her all night without an explanation. If she didn't know, he didn't want to tip her off. Following her like a puppy wasn't an option. She was too smart and would start wondering why he wasn't letting her out of his sight. "You'll be back?"

"Trust me."

He dropped his hold, trust on a short string. "How long?"

"Not long. I want that dance." She hurried out the doors.

He looked at his watch. He considered telling EJ about the turn of events. Instead, he rushed to Hunter, his backup man. "She's here."

"Who's here?"

"Charlie Davies." He shifted from foot to foot. The music's rhythm raced along with his pulse. He had a second chance to find the meth lab, but he had to play his role right. Back to work. Do the job. He reported, "She didn't leave town like we thought. She's here with a date."

Hunter glanced around. "Who's the date?"

"I don't know." Zander glanced at the increasing crowd. Most of them were in law enforcement and public services.

"Listen, I'm going to invite Charlie to stay with me. I need you to hang back in case she leaves with her date instead."

"Sounds good. I'll get right on that." Hunter grabbed more food for his plate and looked at Zander with wide eyes. "What? It's great food."

Zander glanced at his watch. Ten minutes. He tamped down the building doubt in his mind and grabbed a plate as Hunter faded into the mix of people. Finding a chair near the doors, his attention drifted to the crowd. He took a bite of potato salad and glanced at his watch. Twenty-five minutes.

He shouldn't have let her go, damn it.

…

Charlie fished out her credit card and paid the man behind the counter. He had found a gift bag for the handmade glass figurine. "Thank you," she said to the helpful cashier. "I'm so glad you were open this late."

The Asian man nodded. She suspected he didn't speak English.

She rushed out the shop, through the lobby and down the hall, into the conference area. The large lounge was packed with people dressed in beauty. None of them seemed truly happy.

Weaving through the crowd, she stood inside the open doors, looking for Zander.

He sat straighter when their gazes collided.

Heat exploded in her body with his attention. She closed her eyes and absorbed the nuance. His desires made her come alive. How could she break it off with him?

She hustled to his table and handed him the gift bag. "Here."

"What is it?"

"A handmade glass sculpture of a rainbow trout. I figured the Chief probably likes to fish." She stood tall with pride. "His wife will appreciate the craftsmanship and beauty of the glass."

"I'm very thoughtful." He lifted the gift from her hand and brushed a slow kiss on her cheek. Close to her ear, he whispered, "How can I make this up to you?"

She couldn't find her breath. Her hand rested on her chest calming her pulse. She tilted her head and his rough stubble brushed her cheek. This close his body heated her exposed skin. His pleasant aftershave sent tingles down her spine. She closed her eyes. "New aftershave?"

"You noticed." The tone of his whisper dropped. "Have I told you how much I like that dress on you?"

Goose flesh surfaced on her skin with a zing of desire. She wanted his hands roaming over her curves, like they had before. "Thank you."

He withdrew and her body wept. She stared into those deep golden chocolate eyes. "Why are you here tonight, Zander?"

He blinked, shook his head, and rubbed his shoulder. "I know some of these guys."

"How?" She noticed his body shifted from foot to foot.

He shoved a hand in a front pocket. "Let me drop this gift off and we'll have that dance."

"Okay." Something seemed off. "I'll check in with my date, then meet you on the floor."

His wide shoulders dipped and swayed when he strolled away. She couldn't see his behind, but the drape of his jacket over that area was favorable. She bit her lip and tore her attention away from Zander's backside.

What was she doing? She had decided to end it with him, right? He wasn't the homebody type and she wouldn't be happy with another traveling husband.

She hustled through the crowd to the other side of the room where Corbin sat with his buddies. Each had a beer in front of them and loaded plates, except Corbin. He looked up from their conversation with a wide smile. He seemed in his element with these men, the crowd, and the energy. He stood when she approached.

"Hey, where have you been?"

"I found a friend of mine and we were talking." She sat in a chair next to him.

He settled and faced her. "Are you having a good time?"

She shrugged. "There are a lot of people here."

"Yeah, it's a great turnout." He glanced around the room and back at her. He placed his warm hand over hers on her lap.

She glanced at his thick fingers. Solid. Confident. He leaned closer to her and asked, "Are you okay?"

"I guess I'm a little distracted."

"Want to dance?" His light tone brought a smile to her lips.

"Yes." She stood.

He placed a warm hand against her lower back. As they made their way through the crowd Corbin said hello to people he knew. He cradled her in his arms on the dance floor and she followed his lead easily. The soft music held a slow beat.

"You're a good dancer," he said. "Where did you learn?"

"My father taught me. How about you?"

"My ex-fiancé ran a dance studio." He glanced over her shoulder, smiled at someone, and nodded. His attention drifted back to her.

She asked, "How long were you together?"

"A couple of years. How long were you married?"

"A little over a year." Her stomach knotted, and she looked at his shoulder to avoid his eyes. "What are some other things you like to do?"

"I fish."

"Have you fished with the Chief?" She looked back into his eyes. Her gift was right on. She couldn't contain her smile.

Amusement shone in his stare. "He has a nice boat. We've been out a few times. Do you fish?"

She winced at the idea of getting slime on her hands. "Not my kind of thing."

"What's your kind of thing?" His attention drifted over her features. He spun her under his arm, settled her back in place, and smiled.

The tempo of the music changed. Corbin paused, adapted his rhythm, and guided her again. This time, their pace didn't allow for small talk. He twirled her out, in, and took her breath with the stride he set.

Someone tapped her on the shoulder. She looked at a taller woman with brunette hair. "May I cut in?"

Charlie glanced at Corbin and noticed his surprise. She lifted her eyebrows with silent question to him. He shrugged. She stepped to the side for the brunette and said, "I'll go get a drink."

Charlie eased through the crowd, glanced back at Corbin's wide smile, and considered his relaxed demeanor with his new partner. She spotted Zander a few feet from her and decided it was a good time for their dance.

Her heartbeat rushed at the idea of his arms wrapped around her and she frowned. Maybe this wasn't a good idea. She was here to break it off, not encourage the affair. She needed a clear head when dealing with him.

She bit her lip.

He looked at her and smiled. Heated desire lit his eyes when he approached her like a man on a mission. Inches from her, he asked, "Ready for our dance?"

"Yes." She took his offered hand and followed him onto the dance floor. He twirled her into his arms, his attention glued to her features. Heat crawled over her skin when his hot palm caressed the exposed skin on her back. She ran her hand from his chest to his shoulder and held his stare.

She asked, "Did you miss me?"

"Very much." His movements were slower than the rhythm but he hit the right beats in the music. Crowded body to body, he had a controlling hold. "You're driving me crazy in that dress."

His hand cruised up her spine, his fingers curved around her side and under the slip of material. His fingertips caressed the outside of her breast. She leaned closer into him and trembled. His aftershave mixed with desire clouded her control. She hugged her arms around his wide shoulders for balance. "Zander."

"We need to find a quieter place." His warm breath on her neck and shoulder made her blood rush to her lower abdomen.

He quickened the pace, her head spun, and the next thing she knew, he had her by the hand. He turned a couple of corners in an empty hallway before he looked at her again. She glanced at the employee's only plaque on the door.

She resisted, her feet planted to the floor where she stood. "What are we doing?"

"Come on," he coaxed.

"This isn't right."

"You've never done—"

"No!" Surprised by the loudness of her voice, she glanced at no one in the hallway. Then, his lips were on hers and she couldn't think past the thrill. Heat, desire, and logic flew out of her head. She tore her lips from his. "Wait."

"What?" He brushed his hands over his mouth. "What is it?"

"I can't do this."

"I'll be happy to get a room." He winked and smiled. "It's Friday. We could have the weekend together."

Tempted, she ignored the tremble in her body. "No. I don't think so."

"Okay." He stepped closer. "I'll escort you home."

She shook her head. "That's not going to work either."

"What are you talking about?" His eyes searched hers.

The pit of darkness inside her grew with each word. "I think we should break up."

The muscle in his jaw jumped.

"I, ah, this, it's too much for me." She stepped back.

He wrapped a hand around her arm. "Charlie."

"Let me go." She blinked away the tears in her eyes.

He shook his head, cleared his throat, and said, "I can tell you don't want to do this. Why?"

She stepped back. "I have to do this."

"Charlie. Tell me why?" His voice cracked. His posture was less confident. He blinked rapidly and he rubbed his face with his hands. "I don't understand."

"I'm sorry, Zander, I can't." She ran. When she got closer to the party music, she quickly composed herself. She brushed her tears and rushed into the crowd.

...

The words hurt more than he could imagine. He was sunk if he let her go, doomed if he caught her. He rushed back to the party. He couldn't see her in the crowd. His heart pounded as he weaved in and out of groups. He found her at the door with her date.

She kissed the guy on the cheek and headed out the exit. Zander called, "Charlie."

She looked at him and ran.

He took two steps toward her, then spotted Hunter hunched in his jacket outside the window. Hunter signaled. His partner had her covered.

Zander exhaled and rubbed his shoulder while his mind puzzled over what just happened. He had lost it, that's what really happened. He had experienced lust and desire, sure, but nothing like what he felt around her. She made his heart beat faster, his mind lose focus, and his body shift into overdrive.

He mumbled, "I'm so fucked."

"Alexander, is that you?"

He looked at the man Charlie left behind.

The older man approached with a wide smile. His hazel eyes flaked with gold, reminded Zander of his mother. The man's short, darkly sandy hair and muscular stature sucker-punched his thoughts.

"Haven't been called that in a long time." Zander's breath raced from his lungs and he smiled. "Holy shit. Corbin?"

"Hell, yeah, little brother. I didn't think I'd ever find you again." Corbin grabbed him in a hug. "It's so good to see you."

The familiarity sunk into Zander while he hugged his older brother back. After a moment, he shifted away and stared. "I searched for years."

"Damn, you grew taller than me." Corbin had aged well. Barely noticeable wrinkles lined the corner of his eyes. "This is crazy. Let's grab some coffee. Catch up."

He wanted to cheer, shout out his excitement, but remembered he was amongst professionals. He nodded instead. "Sounds great."

Chapter 10

Charlie's lungs burned. Her body shivered when a brisk wind flattened her sweat-soaked shirt against her chest. She glanced up at the storm clouds and sighed. She was on her way to Jordan's Corner store for cat food on her way home from her run. Maybe she would buy coffee too today to warm up too. The thought stirred up memories from the alley fight a week ago and she tamped them down.

She thought about Zander. It was the right thing to do, breaking it off with him. Then why did she feel pain in the pit in her soul?

She approached the corner store, her heart racing from the run. She read the CLOSED sign and threw her hands out. "Really?"

Someone came through the door. It was the tall man she had seen the other day. The man who sang with them. And the man who had plowed the parking lot despite not being paid.

He carried shovels in his arms as he elbowed through the door. One crashed on the ground.

"I'll get that." She rushed to help.

"Thanks." The tall man's smile wrinkled his long face. Charming. She followed him to an old, beat-up Ford with a dirty plow attached to the front.

"So, the store is closed for today?"

He tossed the three shovels in his hands into the back of his open-bed truck. "Closed indefinitely."

Her heart thumped harder against her chest. "What?"

"Mrs. Jordan told us to come and get our stuff."

"I don't understand."

"It's a shame she had to close it. It's a consignment shop for the community. I know others feel the same way. They enjoyed the store as much as I did. The Jordans are good, honest people. Thank you." He took the shovel from Charlie's hands.

He climbed into the cab. "I'll donate these shovels to the local Boys & Girls Club under the Jordan Store name. The boys might be able to get summer jobs working in gardens. They won't go to waste."

"Do you know where … Mrs. Jordan is now?"

"The hospital." He started the truck and handed a card to her. "Thanks for the help. Let me know if I can repay the favor."

"Sure." She glanced at the closed front door and darkened windows of the shop while the old ford puttered off. "Wait, the hospital? What happened?"

The plowman was gone.

Charlie tucked the plowman's business card into her pocket and jogged to the open entry gate of her apartment. She smiled at a man dressed in a uniform with a florist logo.

"You wouldn't happen to be Charlie Davies?"

"I am." Her surprise stopped her entrance into the building.

"These two vases are for you."

She accepted two medium-sized bouquets of flowers. "Thanks."

"Have a great day."

"Wait, I'll get you a tip."

"No need." The man smiled as he darted toward his truck. "Taken care of."

The deliveryman drove off and she shouldered through the door. The bouquets were protected with a film of clear wrap. She studied the different colors until she stepped into the entry mudroom and spotted a pile of taped boxes outside of Milt's closed door. Was he moving? Why?

She climbed the stairs, glancing at the flowers in each hand. The vases were glass. One was square, no-nonsense. The other was tall and bowed out like a fish bowl with a smoke tint. She smiled. Getting flowers were a nice surprise this morning.

A short blonde woman stood in front of Marie's apartment. She wrote something on a clipboard and stuck it to Marie's door. Charlie attempted to pass the woman and read what she had posted when the woman looked at her.

"You're Charlie Davies, tenant in 3C, right?"

Charlie paused. "Yes."

"I'm Suzie Walker, the new superintendent." She looked at her clipboard and scratched the pen on the pad.

"What happened to Milton?"

"He was fired. He wasn't getting the job done." The young woman tore off the top piece of paper.

Charlie accepted the slip between her fingers. "What's this?"

"Eviction notice. You have thirty days to get rid of the cat or you're out."

Her heart hit against her tight chest. "What about Maria?"

"She's three months behind on her rent. She has two weeks to pay or she's out too." Suzie's smile was bright and her perfect ivory complexion blushed in the right places. She blinked bold, long eyelashes over bright blue eyes.

"I'm cleaning up this apartment building. If you'll excuse me, I've got to take stock on the fourth-floor remodel." She hurried down the hall and up the stairs. "Beautiful flowers."

Charlie crumpled the notice between her hand and the vase.

She had grown attached to Shadow and had the adoption paper on the fridge. That meant she needed to move. She adjusted the bouquets into one arm, awkward.

Inside her apartment, she stood at the open front door and adjusted the vases back into her two hands. She looked up and saw her father at the dining table with Beth.

"Hi." Beth's low tone indicated she was angry. She folded her arms, glowering. "Your dad showed up this morning and I let him in."

Charlie slumped her shoulders as her mood dived. "Hi."

"Hey, sweetheart." He stood, closed the door behind her, eased one of the vases from her hands then followed her into the kitchen with it. "I didn't expect your apartment to be so small."

"It's cozy." On her way into the kitchen, she studied Beth's unhappy expression. She set the bouquet on the bar and her father did the same before he sat at the table again. "Nothing like the mansion, but it suits me."

"Does it?" He glanced around. "I guess it's okay."

She expected her father's disapproval when she signed the tenant contract. She figured it really didn't matter. This was what she had chosen.

Her attention drifted down his tailored outfit. The clothes he wore were designed to look casual. He typically paid hundreds of dollars for a t-shirt that looked three years old and pants that seemed like a basement bargain. He had a clean-cut hairstyle with no gray showing his age. His ivory skin was flawless and he kept his chin closely shaven. Cologne mixed in the air with the residual of her morning black tea.

Charlie steady hands started unwrapping the first bouquet.

"I like the security at the front door with the front gate. That's a bonus, huh?" Her father chuckled and sat on the couch. "You could use a few more things for comfort, though."

"I have all I need." The cellophane crinkled in her hands as she wadded it up and she switched to unwrap the second bouquet.

"Where'd you get the flowers?" Beth asked.

"I haven't read the cards yet."

Her father continued, "Maybe some new paint and fixtures."

"I like the fixtures. The paint is new. No need to redo it."

She set the wrapping on the counter. The first bouquet had a dozen red roses with white baby's breath. The mix was fragrant and striking. Corbin's name was on the card. He wrote that he had a good time and wanted another date.

The second bouquet was daisies, lilies and forget-me-nots. Shocked at Zander's name written on the card, she stared for a moment at the signature.

"Well? Who are they from?" Beth emphasized the word who.

"One is from Zander and the other from Corbin."

"And these guys are…?" Her father prompted.

She glanced at him and tucked Zander's card in her pocket. There, the coin rubbed against her fingertips. She wanted to flip it, but didn't want to show it to her father at the moment. "Some friends."

"Peter, your daughter is dating." Beth said.

"Is she?" He smiled. "I'm glad to hear that. I wasn't sure how long it would take her to get over Kenneth. Good to move on, sweetheart."

"That's not all she's doing." Beth emphasized the word *all.*

"Beth." Charlie snapped. "Haven't you said enough?"

"She's been in a alley fight too."

"What?" Peter looked at Beth with raised eyebrows. He looked at Charlie. "Why didn't you call me about this?"

"It was a few days ago."

"Beth, is that why you called me about the money?" Peter exchanged a look with Beth. "Because of all this trouble?"

Beth nodded.

"Money? Charlie looked from Peter to Beth. "What money?"

"It's not surprising." Peter spoke. His features formed a distinguished expression she hadn't seen before. "Look at this place. It's a dump."

Charlie argued, "Just because it's not the mansions on Mercer Island—"

"She's beyond reason." Beth shook her head. "I think she's out of control. Her self-sabotaging needs to stop."

"Beth!" Charlie spoke above Beth's raised voice. "I'm right here. I can speak for myself."

Beth pressed on, "I keep asking her why she's doing this. This place, how she's acting, it's not her. She had things to fall back on when she lived with you. There's nothing here for her this time. I'm worried."

"Enough." Charlie glared. Did Beth really think this about her?

Peter stood and paced the small room. His shoulders jerked while he marched. Agitation laced his tone. "There's nothing wrong with being wealthy."

Beth turned in her chair and faced Peter. "I think she lives in this small, beat-up apartment because she's punishing herself for her failure at her marriage."

"Beth, stop!" Tears surfaced in Charlie's eyes. She couldn't believe the things coming out of her friend's mouth.

Peter froze in mid-step. His attention was glued to Charlie. Beth pressed her lips and stared at Charlie too. Charlie inhaled for calm. She pointed at Beth. "What you just did, what you just said to my father … friends don't do that."

Beth exploded out of the chair. It wobbled on the two legs and finally settled. Beth's blue eyes blazed with anger. "When you say your life is empty, you're missing something, you're unhappy. How do you think that makes me feel? I am your best friend. We spend a lot of time together. Did you not enjoy my company at all?"

Charlie opened her mouth.

"After everything I've done for you, I've been your friend through the worst possible situations, and you don't even help me once." Beth continued, "I can't believe you didn't drop the charges against Marie's family after what I told you."

Charlie didn't know how to respond. She stared at her best friend's reddened cheeks and narrowed eyes.

Beth grabbed a bag from the counter "Sage went to juvenile hall without visitation and Dotty was checked into a mental institution. Maria has no visiting rights at the moment. You couldn't be happy ruining your life. You had to infect others. You had to make everyone see the misery. Well, I'm done. That's all on you now. "

She glared at Charlie and stormed out the door. It slammed it behind her.

Silence rang.

"Shit," Charlie mumbled. She didn't have a clue. Beth's opinion of her sunk in and tied a knot in her chest. Her best friend knew her better than anyone. How could she be wrong about this? Maybe she wasn't. Did Charlie infect others with her negative experiences, the unhappiness?

"You're soaking wet." Peter's tired words twisted her thoughts.

She swallowed, hard. "I was on my way to change."

He nodded and waved a hand. "Take a warm shower too. You don't want to catch cold, sweetheart."

Her chest ached while she processed what Beth said. She stepped into her room and froze at the sight of packing boxes. Half of her stuff was in the boxes, including her bedding. Her body heated for a completely different reason

She moved back into the living area and glared at her father. "What is going on?"

"I never know what you girls are saying half the time. I have no idea what just happened there." Peter shook his head. "I don't understand why Beth is so mad."

"No. Not that." Charlie placed her fists on her hips. "The boxes in my room?"

Shadow shifted in his lap on the couch and Peter stroked the cat's fur. "You're moving back home."

The cold, wet clothes stuck to her shoulders made her shiver while she chose her words and tone carefully. "You don't make this decision for me. You certainly don't start packing my things without my permission."

"I don't need permission." He threw a hand out. "I'm your father."

"You can't make me do what I don't want to do."

"After a few days, you'll thank me. Now, go take a shower." His dismissing behavior reminded her of when she was younger.

She folded her arms. "Get out of my apartment."

He looked at her with raised eyebrows. "Are you talking back to me?"

"I said, get out of my apartment." She pointed at the door.

"Watch your tone, young lady." He stared at her, unflinching. "And you will do what I tell you to do. Go take a shower. We'll leave when you're done."

She took a step toward him. "This is my home. This is my life. I will stay here with or without your blessing. And. You should respect that."

Shadow darted into the bedroom.

Peter stood. His ivory face filled with color. He brushed back his dark hair. "I've shown nothing but respect for you. We both want the same thing. Your happiness."

Her gut tightened. She itched at the skin on her forearms. The splotches of hives weren't there, visually. She pressed her retort through her lips.

He looked at her. "I just don't understand why you're depriving yourself of my money?"

"Your money makes things easy."

"Yeah, Charlie, my money makes things easy. What's wrong with that?"

"It's too easy."

"You're kidding, right?"

She through out her hands. "Money doesn't buy happiness."

"And struggling paycheck to paycheck does?"

"Through the struggle, I'll find happiness." She exhaled and dug deep inside herself for kindness. "Having money just helps to pay the bills. It doesn't … I've got to find…" She paused, tongue-tied.

He threw out his arms. "What? Please tell me what? Is it so bad that I don't want you to live this hard of a life? Why can't you find happiness in luxury?"

He wouldn't understand. She folded her arms. "I just can't."

"My success to make things easier makes you unhappy?" Lines etched in his face from the mid-morning sun through the kitchen window. "All I wanted to do is make sure you're safe, healthy, and able to follow your dreams without—"

"I have to have dreams first." She interrupted.

His attention darted to her. She dropped her arms to her sides.

The soft features on his face contorted into anger. He exploded off the couch and waved his arms around. "Unbelievable!"

"Dad."

He rushed to the door, yanked it open, and stepped into the hall. He turned back with one finger waving at her and wrath in his glare. "I've given you everything you could possibly want so you can follow your dreams without all of this stress. But you throw it right back at me like I'm some monster of a father. I don't understand you, Charlie. I really don't!" He slammed the door.

…

Rebecca's chest constricted as emotion built in her mind and body. Tears welled. She hadn't slept since she knew the truth about the baby and she still wasn't sure how to tell Decker.

She had permanently closed the store. They couldn't make enough to hold open the doors and pay the medical bills. One of them needed a new job. She would tell him today, whatever the cost. It wasn't fair, keeping the truth from him, when he looked forward to working in the store during his rehabilitation.

She got three steps into the hospital when her phone rang. Happy for a distraction, she didn't check the caller identification. "Hello?"

"Ms. Jordan?"

"Mrs."

"Hi, Mrs. Jordan, are you the owner of Jordan Corner Store?"

"Yes." Her heart hit hard against her ribs at the thought of her closed, beloved shop. She had told the people to remove their things yesterday. All her clients had expressed their sadness, but were gracious and understanding.

Tears pooled in her eyes again. She brushed at the rain dripping from her hair and sucked in an uneven breath. "What can I do for you?"

"I liked your video on YouTube. Your voice is angelic."

"YouTube?" She found a bench beside the door and sat. People crossed inside and out in front of her. Tears forgotten for the moment, the breeze was a welcomed flow over her heated skin.

She hadn't thought about the YouTube video since she had talked to a client a few days ago. He mentioned it was trending. Someone had posted the song she sang with Carl and the female customer. "Oh. Yes. The video."

"My name is Steven Beaumont. I work for a small music company and I'd like to talk with you about a recording contract. Is this a good time?"

"Wait, what did you just say?" She focused on his voice.

"If the video is real, and your voice is what I hear, I'm talking about offering you a good amount of money to sing for my company."

Her darkness lightened as she processed the word. The opportunity. A *job*. Tension in her chest released and she smiled.

She wanted to shout, jump, and dance with joy. She sang, "Oh, it's real, Mr. Beaumont. It's real."

...

The hours stretched in Charlie's apartment. Sweet chamomile tea lingered in the comfortable apartment air from the pot in the kitchen. Charlie looked at the time on her phone. Midnight.

Beth hadn't returned to the apartment and didn't answer her messages.

Charlie's involvement in Maria's life had influenced the outcome, Beth was right. The idea of Maria finding her family and separated from them again made her stomach clench. It was her fault.

Her father had never raised his voice until today.

Was she masochistic? Was she a person who finds pleasure in self-denial? Did she find gratification only in pain or humiliation? Did she infect everyone she touched? Her heart clenched and her chest ached. She shook her head.

She needed a change of scene. Her footsteps echoed on the floors as she readied for a walk. Out of tea, she figured she would visit the Green Leaf and Brew. Maybe Lance was working tonight.

She paused before the door, stared at the package on her end table, and decided to take it with her. A late delivery was better than no delivery, right? Charlie locked the door and headed to finish what she had started.

Chapter 11

Charlie slipped the package into her purse. It barely zipped shut. She locked the door behind her. In the hallway, she knocked on Lily's door. Knocked again. Nobody answered and she frowned. She would stop by again after her trip to the Green Leaf and Brew.

She hustled down the stairs, out the door, and through the entry fence. Traffic moved on the street. Waves of tires on water crashed through the city commotion. A few people walked on the street, wearing light coats under the sun. Her sweater protected her body from the cool breeze on her exposed cheeks while she briskly hurried to the bus stop.

After a minute, the bus squealed and clunked to a stop in front of her. A burst of oil mixed with gas settled around her. She smiled at the driver, swiped her city pass along the card reader, and maneuvered to an empty seat.

When the bus stopped at the large transit station, Charlie hurried off and into another bus. It didn't take long to get to the Green Leaf and Brew's strip mall.

The heavy roasted coffee hit her nostrils at the same time she spotted Zander and Lance. They sat at a table for two against the wall, chatting.

Her heart jumped into her throat at seeing him again.

Someone walked into the door behind her.

"I'm sorry I have to do this." Zander stood and reached to his back. He brought a handgun out and pointed it at Lance. In his other hand, he held a shiny badge. "I'm DEA and you're under arrest. Lay down on the ground, hands where I can see them."

A movement behind her jolted her awareness. She glanced back at a man with a gun to her back. "I'm Agent Hunter, Ms. Davies. Show me your hands."

She threw up her hands. She couldn't breathe.

"Good." He turned her away and shoved. "Now, walk forward five feet and lay on the floor."

Lance was pressed to the floor. His body spread. He said, "I knew you were a cop, Zander."

"Keep your hands where I can see them," Agent Hunter's voice boomed from behind her. "Down. Now."

She raised her hands and dropped to her knees. Slowly, she lay on the floor. Her eyes never left Zander as he patted down Lance and drew out a white plastic strip. He tied Lance's wrists together.

Hands patted her down from head to toe then the man behind her yanked her bag off her shoulder. He tossed it toward Zander. His rough hands pulled her arms behind her back and something tied her wrists tightly together.

Zander picked up her purse. He retrieved the package from inside. He set it on the floor between Lance and her. "What's in the package?"

"I don't know," Lance said.

"It's not mine." Charlie said. "I don't know."

"It was in your purse." When Zander tore open the package, Lance sucked in a breath. White powder flew. A gem sparkled.

"Shit!" Lance yelled, "Charlie, what are you doing with that package?"

"It's not my package." Her heart hammered. "It's Lily's. I swear. I had no idea what was inside."

"Lily Wallace?" Lance asked.

Charlie registered Lance's interest. Her body trembled. "You know Lily?"

"She's my drug-dealing sister." Lance mumbled. "This isn't good."

Zander lifted Lance up by the shoulder. His tone was cold. "You trying to tell me that Charlie wasn't delivering this little gem to you?"

"Me?" Lance's tone lifted an octave. "Look, I'm done with all of that. I told my sister to get out too. I don't know anything about this."

Charlie's shoulder hurt when the man behind her lifted her off the floor. She couldn't take her eyes of Zander. Unsettled, she glared at him. "You truly think I'm capable of this?"

He drew out a chair for Lance and shoved him in the seat. "You spent a year in Mexico."

"I was on my honeymoon. Mexico was Kenneth's idea." She winced when Agent Hunter shoved her into a chair opposite Lance. "Call him, ask him, he'll tell you."

Zander stood, arms to his sides, the gun still in his hand. "What about the twenty thousand dollars deposited into your account after you met Lance."

Confusion hit her dead center. "Money?"

"Shit! Twenty grand?" Lance laughed. "Man, this isn't looking good for you, Charlie."

Twenty thousand? She remembered Beth and her father in her apartment. That's what they meant. She closed her eyes and exhaled. "Beth told my father I wasn't doing well on my own. He deposited the money into my account. I had no idea until yesterday."

"Unbelievable." She looked at Zander. "Call my father and I'm sure he'll confirm what I'm saying. What else? I'm an open book. I've never lied to you."

Zander looked away. "When did you meet Lily Wallace?"

"The night you met her. She was playing poker in my apartment. Beth invited her. A few days later I saw her in the hallway. I promised I'd deliver the package to a friend for her. I was going to give it back to Lily today but she wasn't home."

"Oh my God." Lance interjected. He dropped his chin to his chest. "You can't be that naïve. You had to see she was involved in drugs."

"I had no idea. She said she was sick. She had a fever."

Lance scoffed, shook his head.

She caught Zander's attention. "You're undercover?"

"Hell yeah," Lance said. "He's been on me since my wife posted bail five weeks ago. The guy's good. He had me wondering from time to time."

She couldn't look at him anymore. She ducked her head, looked at her shoes. She was a fool, a fool about Lily, and a fool about Zander. The tight restraints couldn't distract from the pain building in her chest, around her heart.

Two men in police uniforms walked into the shop. Zander gave orders to take Lance and her down to the police station. Lance was first to go. Gravity bathed her body. Stuck in time and space, Charlie absorbed the hurt. Zander had betrayed her.

Tears pooled and fell from her eyes. She looked at Zander one last time. His expression was hard. She went willingly into the police car.

Chapter 12

Guilt ate at Zander. Charlie was innocent.

She spent a day in a holding cell while forensic testing confirmed that she hadn't touched the inside of the box. Lily Wallace sobered up and admitted everything Charlie said was right. The package delivery was a favor. The address Charlie was delivering to had been the meth house, but there was no record of Charlie every showing up there.

He personally called Charlie's father, learned that the guy was a control freak. Mr. Davies had put the money into Charlie's account because Beth had mentioned Charlie's money issues.

Zander shook his head. He couldn't stop thinking about Charlie. The memory of tears in her eyes when she was escorted into the squad car made his nightmares. He didn't know what to do about it now. She hated him. She made that clear when she didn't answer his phone calls. He couldn't blame her.

He rubbed the ache in his chest and changed his thoughts to his father. He was guilty for not helping his pop out. He wanted to change that problem.

He sat in the Beats Lounge, and while he waited for Corbin, he dug out his phone. He selected a phone number he hadn't called for a long time, Art Walker.

"Hi, this is Glenda Jones."

"Hi, Ms. Jones, my name is Zander and I'm Milton Green's son."

"Well, hello Zander. You sound very mature. I remember seeing you when you were quite a bit younger. You can call me Glenda. What can I do for you today?"

"I was wondering if I could talk with Mr. Walker."

"Art isn't in the office right now. Would you like to leave a message for him?"

"I was hoping to get a hold of him in person. When will he be back in the office?"

"He's on vacation and isn't due back in office for another week."

"Please, Glenda, my father is about to lose his home along with the only job he's known for years. I think Mr. Walker needs to know the complete story behind the things that happened at Nest Apartments before he actually fires my father."

"Zander, I—"

"I promise, I'll only take the short time I need to talk with him. We can do it on the phone. I'm sure Mr. Walker would agree that Milt is one of the best superintendents he's ever had."

"He was surprised to find out about the drugs. Unfortunately, Art is on a private island. There's no way to reach him electronically."

"If you give me the island location, I can hire a helicopter to take me there. I'll talk with him for twenty minutes tops, and I'll be gone." Zander paused, his shoulder muscles tight with anticipation. Assessing from her silence, Glenda was open to the idea. "Look. Most of what happened circles around my job with the DEA. Do you have deep regrets that you could change about your life, Glenda?"

A exhale came through the phone. "I might get fired for this."

"You might get promoted." He smiled.

"Okay." She rattled off the location of an island in the San Juans. "Good luck."

"Thank you very much, Glenda. You won't regret this." He disconnected and made notes in his phone before he forgot the coordinates.

"Hey, bro."

He smiled. It was so great to have his brother back.

Corbin sat in a chair beside him at the bar. "Good news?"

Helping his Pop was something he could do, something he could make right. He asked Corbin, "How do you feel about helicopters?"

...

A buzz from the entry door blew out of the speaker from the other room. Charlie shuffled through the half-packed boxes to the speaker.

"Buzz me through. I brought Cinnabon." Her father's authoritative tone raked her the wrong way, but she pressed the unlock button.

Charlie ignored the ring of her phone on the bed, grabbed her robe, opened the entry door, and headed to the kitchen for some tea. She set the kettle on the stove by the time her father strolled inside.

He set a box of cinnamon buns on the dining table. "We need to talk."

"Sure." She knew it was coming. She had called him for a ride home from the police station. He had dropped her off without a word or a question about what had happened. She was thankful for his restraint. After spending time in jail, she wasn't excited to face anyone with optimism. "Do you want some tea?"

"If you can afford to spare some."

She glared over her shoulder but grabbed a second cup from the cupboard. The one that said SOME DAYS JUST AREN'T WORTH PUTTING ON A BRA. Shadow meowed at her feet. She fed him and headed to the table with plates. The chair creaked when she plopped down. "Let me get in a few bites before you start, okay?"

"Sure." He headed to the kitchen. "What kind of tea selection do you have?"

"The brands are by the cups."

"What happened to your sweet tea?"

"I ran out."

He grumbled. "I liked sweet."

"Sweet gets boring real fast." She yanked open the bakery box. Hot, sugary smells coursed through her system.

The first bite tempered her sharp tongue, liquefied her strained muscles, and dissolved her worry. The second bite was too damn good. By the third, she looked at her father's pleased expression and laughed with him.

"Some things don't change."

She licked her fingers. "That, we can be thankful for."

He scooped out a roll for himself, took a bite, and moaned at the taste. Silence stretched between them while they enjoyed their breakfast. Peter set his fork down to look at her and she took another roll.

"Ready to start this?" He lifted his eyebrows at her.

She licked her fingers, swallowed her bite. "What do you want to know?"

He leaned forward. "What kind of trouble are you in?"

She shrugged. "I got this coin."

The coin sparkled when she set it on the table in front of him. He picked it up, turned it in his fingers, and looked at her again.

"It's magical." He opened his mouth, she held up her hand. "The etching on the coin changes when I flip it. I didn't flip it last night after you picked me up so I could show you. See where it says VOLUNTEER FOR A TASK?"

She took the coin from him and tossed it in the air. The shadows of the ornate surface compelled her. The gold glittered with the end-over-end movement. The coin landed in her palm. The familiar warmth cruised from her palm to her elbow. Without looking, she handed it back to her father.

He glanced at the coin a moment, then back at her.

"I do the things on the coin." She told him about the cat on the first night and how that led to cleaning the city and singing in public. The coffee for homeless piqued his interest. She told him about baking with Maria and taking out the trash too. Why leave anything out?

"You cooked without burning?" He smiled, eyes alighting with her adventurous story.

"And I enjoyed it," she admitted. "But I botched it all up."

She continued with her story. Her memory of brightening a child's day with Beth knotted her stomach. She missed her best friend. It took her a moment to remember she gave up her seat for the pregnant woman on the bus. "Then I wrote a letter of recommendation for the landlord here. I slipped it under the door because he wasn't home. Turns out he was fired from his job."

She inhaled before she went into volunteering for a task. Her voice shook when she talked about Zander. She couldn't believe he thought she was a drug dealer. Tapping down the pain in her heart and finishing the story, Charlie picked up another Cinnabon roll for comfort. The sweet bite eased some of her anxiety.

"Well, that's quite a story." Peter sat back, rubbed his clean-shaven chin. "Sounds like you could use a day off of everything. How about we take the day together, go for a walk?"

She shrugged. "Fine."

He stood with his plate. "Go get dressed."

Charlie took her time getting dressed, not wanting to face the world. She wasn't looking forward to the day. Beth hadn't returned her calls, probably still angry with her.

She didn't blame Beth. Charlie had enough time to rethink her actions when she was in jail and understood Beth's position. She could see where her actions seemed like self-sabotage.

She shook her head and twisted her hair into a loose knot on her head then buttoned her blouse. Maybe Beth was right about her leaving Peter's house too. Maybe she needed adult supervision because she couldn't control the impulses.

She truly didn't know now. The emptiness inside her chest expanded.

She lifted the phone from the bed where she had discarded it this morning. Zander had left messages, but she didn't want to see him again. The coin collector, Greg Strike, had left two messages.

Her body trembled at the idea of going out when she was raw emotionally. Usually, she would binge on ice cream until the human part of her surfaced. Did it matter? She exhaled, straightened her clothes, and exited the bedroom.

Her father looked at her from the kitchen. "Ready?"

She realized something was missing. Her steps to the kitchen were slow while she catalogued the things in her space. He had put the cinnamon rolls away and cleaned up the table. She glanced at the bar. Then it hit her. One of the flower bouquets was gone.

"Dad, did you do throw out a bouquet?"

"No."

She stood beside the flowers. Corbin's bunch was the one missing. The card sat in the place of the vase. "Any idea what happened to them?"

"Sorry, no." He walked to the living area. "Let's go."

"Who would take my flowers?"

"I don't know. If you leave your door open enough—"

"I don't leave my door open all the time." She closed her eyes and reined in her irritation. It wasn't his fault her life was a mess. "Where are we going?"

"Just let me kidnap you for today. I guarantee we'll have a good one."

This was a game they used to play when she was younger. She would play hooky at school or work and he would spoil her with trips or gifts. In her mood, she wasn't sure if the idea was good or bad.

Whatever. She pocketed the coin, shouldered her purse, locked the door behind her, and then headed towards the staircase.

Someone exited Maria's apartment. The shorter woman was sobbing. When she glanced up, Charlie's heart raced and she hurried to the woman. "Dottie? Are you okay?"

Dottie looked at Charlie for a moment. Her red-rimmed eyes were puffy and filled with tears. Her cheeks were clean like her clothes, her jacket too. Very different from when Charlie had given her a cup of coffee in the alleyway. Dottie seemed … functional.

"You're the woman from the alley?" Dottie sniffed.

Charlie nodded. She smiled. "How are you?"

Dottie's features pinched in a painful expression.

Charlie wanted to hug the woman, but she sensed Dottie didn't want physical comfort right now. Instead, Charlie tangled her fingers together.

"How am I?" Dottie sniffed again. "I have to live in a strange house with lots of other women and a nurse and a shrink. I have to pee in a cup everyday. Did you know that? Do you know what that's like?"

Her recent ugliness of being in jail surfaced. She empathized with lost freedoms. Charlie's fingers tightened together. "I'm—"

"My son is everything to me!" Dottie screeched. "You couldn't understand. You don't have children." She shoved past Charlie. "My life is ruined. I should never have taken that coffee from you that day. Next time you want to help a homeless woman, why don't you kill her instead? That would be more humane."

Charlie's guilt smacked her in the ribs and vibrated throughout her body. She reached a hand out to Dottie.

Dottie headed down the stairs. She stopped on the second one. Tears fell off her cheeks and dribbled onto her jacket. "He's a good boy. He really is. He didn't deserve that. I didn't either. We didn't do anything to you. Damn you!"

"Dottie."

"Don't ever talk to me again." She shook her head and hurried down the stairs.

Charlie took a few steps after Dottie and stopped. Best to leave it alone despite her urge to make things better. She didn't look at her father, didn't want to see whatever expression might be on his face.

She stepped outside. A black car was double-parked on the street before them.

"Here's our ride." Her father's hand landed on her lower back and he steered her through the gate, and into the car. "Are you okay?"

Charlie nodded, her mind wallowing. Peter settled next to her and told the driver to go.

"How long are you in town for, Dad?"

"As long as it takes."

"What takes?" She looked into his brown eyes.

"I need to make sure my daughter is okay." He glanced out the window. A muscle in his narrow chin flexed. Peter was slim in appearance but bold in temperament. He had raised his voice to her two days ago, which shocked her because he didn't need to most of the time. Using the right words was his forte.

Her gut twisted and tension raised in her shoulders. She itched at the skin on her forearms. The splotches of hives weren't there.

Peter's phone rang. He fished out the device and engaged in a business conversation. She hated making him tired and worried.

Charlie fished out the coin from her pocket and read the next task.

Go BUNGEE JUMPING. 11/21

The weight on her shoulders increased. There was no way she could do that.

She looked at her father on the phone. His eyes had dark bags and he seemed ten years older than before. He was right. He didn't deserve to see his daughter in the destitution he had worked so hard to avoid.

Truth was, she had the same problem, with or without the money. Her struggle was for nothing. The hollowness still loomed inside her body, her life.

She looked at the golden coin in her hand. Her finger and thumb rubbed the crude surface. Nothing had come from her singing in Jordan's Corner store. Sure, she had overcome a childhood fear, but that was a hollow victory because she felt terrible about the closing.

Dottie was right. She had lost her son because of Charlie's involvement.

Charlie had made a friend in Maria when they made cookies. Unfortunately, Charlie couldn't see Maria talking with her after what was done.

Beth... Charlie's chest tightened more. Her gut knotted with the memory of Beth's emotional tirade in the apartment. The thought of losing Beth's friendship added to the growing abyss inside herself.

Lance was likely in jail right now, with his sister, because of the damn package Charlie had contributed to Zander's investigation.

Zander ... She couldn't go there. The pain was too great. She loved him and he had used her.

Maybe she was too far gone. She couldn't change her ways. Her experiences with the coin were only adding depth to the problem. She exhaled, ignored the tears escaping her eyes and said, "I need to make a stop at the Bellevue Rare Coins store, then I'll do whatever you want."

...

Art Walker's vacation home was located on Cheshire Island, a private island in the San Juan chain. Art had a fondness for "Alice In Wonderland." Things on the island were named after things in the story.

Zander stood in Hole Hall, staring out the window at the angry sky. Without cell coverage, the remote island seemed like a prison. He couldn't get Charlie's defeated expression out of his head. Thinking about her tears killed him. His shoulder hadn't stopped hurting since he watched her climb into the police car.

He cleared his throat, tried to clear the pressure in his chest. "When did you say this storm was going to lift?"

"We haven't even talked with Mr. Walker and you're wanting to leave the island?"

Zander glared at Corbin. "I need to get back."

Corbin laughed and gestured with his hand at the empty padded chair next to him against the wall. "Sit down, little brother. You're making me nervous. Who's the woman?"

"I guess this is as good a time as any to tell you." Zander rubbed his hand through his hair and kept far away from Corbin.

"Tell me what?"

"I think I'm in love with Charlie Davies."

Corbin's laid-back expression pinched. His shoulders shifted back and his chest expanded to a formidable width. "Excuse me. Did I hear you right? Charlie? My Charlie? The woman I'm dating? How do you know her?"

Zander dug his heels into the floor despite the urge to run. "We've been seeing each other for a while now. We danced at the Chief's party."

Corbin stood and approached with measured steps. "I should knock all of your teeth out right now for not telling me earlier."

"I was undercover on a drug case when we met." He told Corbin as much as he could about the meth house and his misdirected trust. "I didn't want to fall for her. It just happened."

Corbin grabbed a handful of Zander's shirt. "You little punk. You put Charlie through all of that and left her in jail, without another word?"

Zander contained his instincts. This was his brother. He didn't want to fight him.

Nose to nose, Corbin opened his mouth again, but someone came through the door causing him to drop his hold.

Zander breathed in relief. He straightened his shirt.

"This isn't over," Corbin's gruff tone reflected in his stiff posture.

"Well, what a nice surprise, Zander my boy." Art Walker entered the room. "I haven't seen you in years. Shit, look how you've grown."

In a black trench coat with a checkered cravat, Art Walker was shorter than Corbin. He had gray hair under a red top hat. There was a natural curve to his back. His hands shook when he patted Zander's shoulder. He held out an open palm to Corbin. "Who is this?"

"Corbin Black." His brother's low tone sharpened Zander's awareness. "I'm the pilot."

"Good to meet you." Walker glanced out the window. "Looks like this storm is going to last the night."

"Just our luck," Corbin said.

Zander caught a cold stare from Corbin and covered the shiver that ran up his spine by shoving his hands in his front pockets.

"Well." Walker gestured to the door. "Why don't you boys join me for dinner?"

Walker led the way into a hall. The floor was red carpet and cards were painted on the walls. Each card had a series of hearts scattered in the square. Eerie music cut in and out of the air. The high ceilings awed Zander. At the black door, the end of the hall, Walker entered another room.

Corbin lifted his eyebrows and whispered to Zander. "Interesting."

Zander nodded and followed his older brother inside.

This room had a black-and-white checkered floor. Mismatched doors were located on each wall. The octagon space fit a long table with a white cloth and small sandwiches. A tea set was spread among other food. Savory spices filled the air.

Walker took a seat at the head of the table, Zander sat to his right and Corbin sat to his left. Zander couldn't shake his discomfort.

"I'm really hoping the storm clears," Corbin said.

"I like the storms." Walker said. He started serving himself from the food on the table.

Zander's stomach grumbled despite his resistance to the dainty buffet. He grabbed a few flower-looking things, some green leafy stuff, and a slab of meatloaf. That's what he thought it was and he wasn't going to ask. "I came here to discuss my father's situation with you, Mr. Walker."

"Call me Art."

Zander glanced at Corbin. The formal space seemed awkward for casual manners, but he shrugged. Zander continued with his report. He concluded with, "Milt runs a good building. You'll lose a valuable asset."

Art nodded. "I was surprised to find out what was happening."

"If it helps ..." Zander liked the flower-shaped things. They were fruity. He swallowed his bite. "I'll be around for a year or so. I've put in for leave. I'll help Milton improve his security and interviewing procedures."

"Do you know I have a granddaughter? Her name is Suzie. She's about your age."

Zander looked at Corbin, exchanged a puzzled look, then looked back at the aging man. "No, I didn't know."

"See, she needs to learn business. She loves that old building."

Zander nodded understanding. Art intended to fire Milt and give the building to Suzie. "How about Milt and I take Suzie under our wings. We'll teach her what we know. This way the building will continue to generate money and Suzie gets a good education."

Two men entered the room dressed in black and white stripped shirts. Their black pants matched too. Each thin man had a baldhead. One carried a silver tray with a white letter on it. He set the tray next to Art and exited the room with his twin as quietly as they entered.

"Excuse me." Art set down his silverware and picked up the envelope. He fished out the letter inside, unfolded it, and lifted a pair of glasses from his pocket to read. After a moment he asked, "Do either of you know a Charlie Davies?"

Corbin sat straighter. "Charlie and I dated for a while. She's the reason Zander and I are here together today."

Zander thought for a moment. If she hadn't been Corbin's date and his suspect, the search for his brother would have taken longer—if he had found him at all. Another reason to love that woman. He was forever thankful. He nodded his agreement.

"Why do you ask?"

Art looked at Corbin. "Is she Peter Davies's daughter?"

Corbin glanced at Zander, Zander nodded, Corbin confirmed with Art. "Yes. That's her."

"This is a letter of recommendation from her." Art set the letter back onto the tray and settled deeper into the chair. "I haven't seen Peter in years. That man is a genius when it comes to technology. Not to mention his skills in negotiating a contract. I imagine his daughter would be smart as a whip."

"Charlie lives in the building."

Art looked at Zander. "Does she?"

Zander nodded.

"See, I'd like to get to know Peter again." Art tipped up his hat, scratched his forehead, and rested his fingers on his lips for a moment. With a pointed finger he said, "I'll make you a deal."

Chapter 13

Zander trudged out of the room shaking his head. He slept terribly. From Corbin's threatening attitude to the strange mushroom bed, he couldn't shut his mind down all night. He didn't get a chance to talk with Corbin about Charlie after the meal because Art had a performance company on the island.

The small theater room had a stage where actors and actresses presented a live performance of *Alice The Shrinking Woman.* It was an independent story, fan fiction, written by the company's director. Art Walker loved the director.

Zander had said his goodbye to Art after dinner last night. They exchanged contact information and Art insisted on a monthly report concerning the improvements made on the apartment building.

Corbin said to meet him at the helicopter this morning, and to be ready to fly.

Zander glanced at his watch while he rushed through a hall painted like a mole cave. He ducked some stringy things, roots from the surface world. He had to laugh or grumble. The place was exotic and creepy. He chose laughter.

Relieved, he broke through an outside door.

The humid air lifted his spirits. Sun peeked through a light splatter of clouds. The idea of staying another night at Art's Fun House did not sit as well as the idea of keeping Charlie in the building for Milt's benefit.

How was he going to do it?

Zander didn't believe Charlie wanted anything to do with him. The look in her eyes when she was escorted to the car was clear. He knew. She had loved him and he had hurt her. He didn't blame her, but to his defense, he had fallen for her the same way she had fallen for him.

Could she love him again? Could she forgive him?

His mind circled around the questions while he rushed down a grassy hill. In the distance, he spotted Corbin checking the helicopter on the concrete landing pad. Zander smiled. It was good to see his brother. Now, his motivation to find his second brother jumped high on his priority list.

"Good morning," Corbin greeted him with a smile and a gesture at the helicopter. "Ready to get the hell out of here?"

Zander chuckled.

Twenty minutes into the one-hour flight, Corbin said, "So, what are we going to do about the Charlie situation? She's a good woman. I can't believe the way you treated her. She has innocent written all over her. She's so sweet. She makes my teeth hurt."

Zander exhaled. "I know. I was a idiot."

"You said you loved her. Is that true?"

"I really messed things up, but, yeah, I love her." Zander looked out at the water and small boats below them.

"I love her too."

Zander snapped his attention to his brother's profile. The sun highlighted his blondish hair. Apparently, the crooked nose was hereditary. "You plannin' on askin' her to marry you?" He pressed the last word—*too*—between his lips.

Corbin shrugged and didn't look at him.

He hadn't thought about how deep Charlie and Corbin were into their relationship. His stomach burbled at the idea of Charlie with someone else. That someone being his big brother…!

Zander adjusted in his seat. The damn thing wasn't big enough.

When Corbin landed the copter, Zander spotted Beth next to a car.

Corbin rushed to Beth, picked her up in his arms, and twirled her around.

Zander hurried beside them. He folded his arms, then glowered at the laughing couple. "What happened to Charlie?"

Corbin returned his glare. "I couldn't let you get away with what you did to her that easily. She's a good woman. And I had fun making you squirm."

"What?" Zander couldn't contain his relief. "You were messing with me? You're not really in love with Charlie?"

"Naw. I went to a bake sale for the YWCA and saw this lovely treat behind a stack of yummy cookies." Corbin looked at the blonde with adoration in his eyes.

"It was love at first sight," she said, then flashed the ring in the sunlight.

"I thought—" Zander absorbed the rush of relief as he hugged his brother. "You had me going there, bro. Congratulations."

"Thanks."

"Now, give me a second. I've got to make a call."

Corbin laughed. "Sure thing, little brother."

Zander dug out his phone, inhaled the fresh air, and left a new message for Charlie. He turned to Beth. "Do you know where Charlie is?"

"I haven't seen her for a couple days. The cat is gone from the apartment too."

His shoulder ached with his concern. "Have you talked to her on the phone or anything? I've left messages she hasn't returned."

"I've been avoiding her." Beth confessed. She hooked her hand in Corbin's. Some of the excitement and happiness in her expression drained. "I haven't decided how to tell her about our engagement yet."

Chapter 14

Peter arranged an interview for Charlie, at her request. The company had offered huge incentives to her to join their staff as the CFO. If the company continued on the upward trajectory it was on, she would make a six-figure income. If she was busy, she figured, she couldn't mess up anyone else's life with her self-destructive behavior.

"Hello, Mrs.—"

"It's Ms. Davies," Charlie interrupted.

The tall blond man shook her hand. "My name is Luke Atwood. I am the CEO of the Dragon Game and Development Corporation." He nodded to a man beside him. "And this is my assistant, Gage Thomson."

"Hello." She shook each man's hand, then sat. Cups of coffee in hand, they took seats inside a local bakery.

"Your father told us that you're currently looking for a job," Atwood began.

She nodded, intertwined her fingers together on her lap like a good girl. She was well qualified for the position.

Mr. Atwood flipped through some pages in front of him. He looked at her and continued, "We'd like to share our company vision with you to see if you're interested in our CFO position."

She didn't need the show. It didn't matter if she liked the company. She had given up on being happy last night when she told her father she wanted to move back in with him. She retrieved her cat and gave Beth the apartment. Well, she would give Beth the place once she talked with her again. She hoped it would be soon.

"As you can imagine," she said to the CEO, "with my father being a close friend, he gave me plenty of information about your business and your future objectives." She failed to read through it all. "I'd like to discuss the offer today, if you don't mind. I'd like to get back to work as soon as possible."

Chapter 15

Charlie dreamed. Inspiration bloomed her imagination, made her feel alive, made her want to live there, forever, in that satisfying moment where she made all the rules. Anything could happen. It was up to her. All she had to do was—

"Ms. Davies?" His familiar voice snapped her out of the fantasy like a cracked whip on a workhorse's back.

She groaned and rolled onto her side, away from the doorway where the butler stood. "What is it?"

"You're late for your run."

"So?"

"You don't want to be late for work."

After her run, she had breakfast with her father and then went off to work. This was her second day back in her father's house, but the routine had remained the same. "Okay, Steve, okay."

The old man left without another word.

She didn't have anything against the butler other than the fact she couldn't remember a day in childhood where he didn't wake her up from her ideal dreams. She petted Shadow, who was stretched on the overstuffed pillow next to her, and yanked the thick comforter off dreading her mindless schedule ahead.

Slumped at the table, she squinted at the beautiful arrangement of fresh flowers from the gardener. They were sunflowers and daisies today. Each day, Steve made sure the arrangements were perfect.

Her eggs were perfectly cooked, her bacon was perfectly crisp, and she was perfectly bored before 7 a.m.

Fifteen minutes later, she squeezed into her jogging suit and tied her laces. Her shoe-covered feet hit wet sidewalk by 7:45. The clouds didn't dim the details of the neighborhood houses while she passed by.

The houses were beautiful, all professionally landscaped. The streets were clean. People waved as if she knew them. And everything seemed right as the rain that nobody could stop.

She liked the suburb well enough. She had grown up on Mercer Island, but part of her didn't fit. The part that wanted …

something. Something more. Something to fill the void in her chest. Something worth getting out of bed for in the morning.

She shook her head. Old habits were hard to break. She inhaled deeply to expand the cramped muscles around her lungs and headed back to the house. She circled around to the back porch and spotted her father at the table.

As always, Peter was dressed in a casual suit. He sipped from his cup while she accepted a bottle of water from Steve. The butler handed her a towel too.

She drank half the bottle before she looked at her father.

He grinned from ear to ear. "Are you excited to start your new job, Charlotte?"

"I've asked you before to call me Charlie."

"I named you Charlotte and Charlotte is what I'll call you. I like the name."

"Well, I think it sounds old. It's the name of a stubborn man-hater."

He laughed. "Man-hater? That's not what I had in mind when I named you. I thought it sounded classy."

She shook her head. "Anyway, what did you ask me?"

"Are you excited to start your new job?"

"As I'll ever be."

Peter took a bite of his toast.

In the silence, Charlie looked out at the view. The house stood on a hill where she saw the tops of other homes and beyond, the blue water of Lake Washington. The serenity counteracted her dread.

"I'm breaking the merger with Kenneth today." Her father said.

She looked at him. "You shouldn't."

"I don't want to work with him." He waved a hand.

She set her empty bottle on the table and wiped sweat from her forehead. "Sometimes personal feelings get in the way of great business."

"I don't care." He dropped his napkin on the table over his food. "I can't work with someone who isn't loyal."

"Dad, you don't need to do this because of me."

He waved his hand again and stood. "It's practically done."

She exhaled. "I think you should reconsider. Take another look at the projected financial outcome. Kenneth's business is right on track. You'll both make money if you give him the recipes your company has been working on for new fireworks. You are both bright, but together, you could be brilliant." Internally she smiled at her intended pun.

"Well, I don't like him."

She nodded agreement. "We work with people we don't like when it's business and it makes sense."

Expressionlessly, he looked at his watch. "Better get going. You don't want to be late on your first day of the new job." His enthusiasm raked along her eardrums. "I'll see you at Frankie's for lunch."

She pressed her lips and headed back to her room to get dressed.

In the past, he had liked to talk about his negotiations from his morning meetings at lunch. He had admitted that telling her about his business problems helped him strategize the solutions. Not that he took her suggestions. Just that she was a good listener.

She exhaled. She couldn't get mad at him for assuming they would fall into the old routine. He liked his routine and it was her choice to come home.

She had no one to blame for her despair but herself.

She finished dressing and headed out the door where she met Steve. "Hello."

"Good morning." He was dressed in a black shirt and black pants. He had a full head of gray hair and bright blue eyes. "Off to work, Ms.?"

"Yes." He would never call her Charlie. He kept things on a professional level the entire time she grew up.

In the car, her phone vibrated. The caller was identified as Zander. She blew out a huff. He needed to get a clue. She was done with his type of man. The type of man that would say "I love you" only to get what he wanted. No doubt he got a promotion for busting the case.

Charlie's gut twisted at the idea of Lance in a cell because of her stupidity. Lance had wanted out, that's what he had said when they arrested him. She hadn't heard from him or Lily since the bust.

She had returned for Shadow to find her apartment building half empty. Notices stuck everywhere. Boxes in the hallways. Milt was nowhere to be seen. She had messed up everyone and everything on her little adventure. Beth wasn't talking to her, either; there had been no response to Charlie's voice messages.

Tears threatened her control. The car stopped and she inhaled. She needed to leave it alone. She cared about all of them and didn't want to hurt them anymore. Anything she likely did would ruin the rest of their lives.

She imagined Maria, alone, God knows where.

Today, she was scheduled to attend orientation. Luke Atwood wanted her to mingle with the next wave of hires. She would sign her employment contract after.

She thought about her desk, the digital ledgers, the long hours of crunching numbers for the company. The details didn't matter. The job was the same.

Her heels clacked on the cement at her feet while she marched inside the tall building. She maneuvered around the morning work crowd with ease. Strong perfume wafted with men's cologne. The walls enclosed her in a nice little box. Nonsensical chatter echoed in the entry space, and she joined the line for the elevator.

Moving slowly from floor to floor, she watched the light above the heads on the elevator door. She took a step back, then headed for the stairs.

She shoved through the third-floor door and paused as she saw a man on the floor, dressed in white. He hummed while he ran a paint roller along the wall. She couldn't see earplugs in his ears or hear music on the floor, but he started to dance while he painted.

She shifted and he looked at her from over his shoulder. "This floor is closed, ma'am. I can't have you wandering around in here."

"Okay. Sorry." She turned back to the door.

"No problem." He filled his roller again with paint in a pan and began dancing and humming again. He seemed cheerful, here, alone, working. His feet maneuvered as if he were tap dancing, then he looked at her again. A chunk of blond hair fell into his green eyes. "Is there something I can help you with?"

She asked, "Why are you dancing?"

He chuckled. "I woke up this morning and my granddaughter made me breakfast in bed."

Charlie lifted her eyebrows with a silent question.

The man set his roller down, faced her, and smiled. "See, my son left his daughter on my doorstep when she was a baby." He chuckled. "Taking her in was a hard adjustment for me for me. I felt like my son was screwing up my retirement."

"Anyway, my granddaughter and I had a fight two days ago. She was making a mess of her life, failing out of school. It all came to bite me in the ass, my resentment toward my son. I called her a burden."

He shook his head then placed a hand on the door.

"She threatened to leave and I realized I'd probably have one foot in the grave if she wasn't testing my will. I was wrong. She wasn't bad for me. I'm counting my blessings that she stuck around to make me breakfast today despite what I said."

He swung the door open and winked. "If you don't mind, I need to get back to work."

Charlie nodded. She stepped into the stairwell.

The door closed between them.

She stared at it.

Something was happening here. She didn't quite know what, but she couldn't move. She turned towards the stairs. If she continued up she would meet her destiny, the path of least resistance.

Why wasn't she rushing toward it?

She wanted to stop screwing things up. She hated putting everything on the line, her friends, her father, and her happiness. The risk was too great.

The painter had risked his grandchild. He could have given her to child services, but he didn't. Deep in his heart, he knew, that without risk nothing changed. He needed a change. His granddaughter kept him alive through her shenanigans.

The past few weeks, Charlie had forgotten about her pathetic existence. She had thrown caution and consequence to the wind and lived.

But she hated feeling … feeling. Last week, Beth had asked her why she put herself through all the pain.

She remembered her reply: *"I'd rather the feel pain than nothing at all."*

Things weren't perfect, like they weren't perfect for the painter, but through it all she had more enrichment than ever before. She fished out her phone and played the first voice message from Zander.

"Charlie, I know I'm the last person you want to see right now." He seemed tired. His voice was thick and low. "But I can't stop thinking about you. Please give me a call so we can talk about this. I don't think I can sleep until I see you again."

The phone rang in her hand. Her heart jump-started and she connected the call.

Beth said, "Charlie, where are you?"

"Beth? I thought—"

"You need to get back here right away. I need your help. Please hurry home."

Her heart sprinted at the panicked tone in Beth's voice. She started down the stairs. "I'm on my way."

Chapter 16

Charlie climbed out of the car in front of the Nest Apartments.

She had called her father to cancel lunch.

She exhaled and walked through the security fence. In the mudroom, she met Suzie right outside Milt's old apartment. Suzie smiled. "Hey, haven't seen you around. I thought you moved out with your cat."

"I did." The affirmation dried Charlie's mouth. She headed to the stairs. "I'm visiting my friend."

Milt came through the apartment door behind Suzie with his wide shoulders and dark skin. Charlie froze at the bottom of the stairs and watched Milt smile at Suzie. "Ready to get…" He glanced at Charlie. His grin widened. "Hey!"

Happiness boiled inside her and overflowed. She ran to him, gave him a big hug, and inched back to smile. "I'm so glad to see you."

"Me too." He shoved his hands in the front pockets of his jeans pockets. "I wanted to say thank you."

She dropped her arms to her sides and glanced from him to Suzie then back in shock. She had expected him to glower at her because of the cat. Instead, he was thanking her. "What are you talking about?"

"Suzie is the owner's granddaughter and she wanted experience in the management business. Your letter of recommendation swayed the owner into giving me my job back so I could teach her. To make a long story short, meet my new assistant." He gestured to the blonde. "Suzie Walker."

Suzie nodded. "After having a taste of working this building on my own, I'm happy to step back and learn how it all works. It's harder than it looks."

Charlie's chest expanded with the news. Her letter had helped Milt gain his job back. She wouldn't have thought to write the letter without the coin. "I'm so glad you're back. This is where you need to be."

"Thanks." He stepped around her. "We are headed to Maria's apartment to help her move."

"Okay." Charlie nodded. "I'll follow you up. I'm visiting Beth."

They jabbered about the business and Charlie half listened. When they stopped at Maria's door, they said their goodbyes and Charlie continued to the last apartment on the level. What was now Beth's apartment.

She didn't know if she should knock or walk in. Her body trembled in decision. She didn't want another fight with her best friend.

The door opened and Beth stood in front of her. For a moment, Charlie thought she would hear an earful of resentment from Beth. However, Beth threw her arms wide and cheered, "You're here!"

Charlie's uneasiness settled a little while they hugged. First the warm welcome from Milt. Now Beth was happy to see her, hooking her elbow to guide her into the apartment.

"Thanks for coming, Charlie."

"Absolutely." Charlie glanced around. Nothing had changed except that Beth's luggage wasn't cluttering up the living space. Beth looked wonderful. Her ivory skin glowed, her makeup was perfect, and her yellow shirt dripped seductively off her slim shoulders. "What's the urgency all about?"

"Here, on the table, I need a decision by the end of the day and I can't figure it out. White or ivory lace?"

Charlie stopped beside the table and studied the wedding magazines spread over the surface. Models were dressed like brides. She eased into an open chair at the table. "I don't understand."

Beth held out her hand. She wore a beautiful engagement ring.

Charlie's heart filled with joy and excitement for her friend. She hugged her, but Beth's body was stiff. Charlie eased back into the chair. "Is this the guy you met at the bake sale a few weeks ago? The one you said was different from the other guys you dated?"

"Yes." The color in Beth's cheeks drained. She inhaled deeply and sat in a chair next to Charlie. Beth placed her hand on top of Charlie's. "I'd like to introduce you to him. Do you mind?"

"Not at all."

Beth inhaled again then called, "Corbin, honey, can you come out here for a minute?"

Charlie's skin heated. "Corbin?"

Corbin stepped out of the living room in jeans and no shirt. His chest was more muscular without a shirt. He yawned, stretched, and blinked as if Beth had woken him from a deep sleep. When he locked eyes with Charlie, her heart flipped.

"Hey," his deep voice held concern. "Beth told you, huh?"

"My Corbin?" Charlie stood. Her heartbeat kicked into overdrive. "I can't believe this. The guy you met at the bakery was my Corbin?"

Beth's attention didn't quite meet Charlie's eyes.

Corbin smiled, shifted to the table, and sat in a chair next to Beth. "It was love at first sight."

"Why didn't you say something at the steakhouse?" Charlie stepped backwards towards the front door. "You could have said something."

"It was to early to say anything." He shrugged and placed his hands over Beth's shaky fingers. "Besides, you were preoccupied with Maria."

"Why didn't you tell me, Beth?" Charlie's disbelief mixed with her happiness and frustration about the deception. "All this time and I thought you were with Maria."

"I … I felt bad once I figured it out … I took the bouquet he gave you because I was jealous and that's when I knew I did really like him. I didn't know how to tell you."

Charlie's head spun. She wasn't sure if she was happy, sad, or angry. She shook her head and opened the door. "I need to get some air."

"Hi." Zander's wide frame blocked the exit.

Charlie's heart flipped. She stumbled back and tripped. She fell onto the couch. Her breath caught in her throat. Heat engulfed her body at seeing him again. He looked incredible in jeans and a long-sleeved shirt. She didn't know what to say when he stepped inside closing the door behind him.

"Hey, man!" Corbin stood from the table, rushed across the room, and gave Zander a strongman hug. "Good to see you, little brother."

Charlie gasped. "Brothers?"

"Yeah, Zander is my brother." Corbin smiled from ear to ear. "We met that night at the Chief's anniversary party after you left."

She didn't know what to say. Nervous energy played with her emotions. She folded her arms and glanced at Beth's sad face at the table. "You knew about this too?"

"No." Beth said. "Not until they went to the Walker's island last weekend. Corbin told me about it on the phone."

"You had coverage the entire time we were on the island?" Zander punched Corbin in the shoulder, but had a smile. "You knew I wanted to call Charlie."

Corbin shrugged. "You needed time to figure out why you wanted to call her."

"Yeah. I guess I did." Zander looked at her.

She lifted her cool palms to her heated cheeks. What was happening here? The information was blasting at her fast. She comprehended the facts, unfolding. Unfortunately, her emotions were strung too tight for her to accept what was happening.

Corbin sat on the couch and took her hands in his. "We have to thank you. Finding one of my brothers is awesome. I'm not sure I could have done it on my own. Definitely not this fast. And for bringing Beth and I together. She told me that you helped Maria bake those cookies for the YWCA that night. Otherwise, Maria wouldn't have been there with Beth. We wouldn't be engaged right now. I'm happier than I've ever been. I owe it to you."

"Lucky me." Charlie's sarcasm dripped off her lips with the mumble.

"No."

She looked at Zander.

"Lucky me." He shifted to the couch, eased to sit next to her. Corbin went to Beth and kissed her on the cheek. Zander's eyes held her captive while he spoke. "I'm so sorry." He stabbed his fingers through his hair and looked at Corbin.

Corbin cleared his throat. "Um, we'll go for a walk."

Corbin escorted Beth out of the apartment.

The door closed and Zander changed his focus onto her. "The case unfolded, Lily confirmed what we already knew, and you were innocent in it all. You'll likely be called in to give a statement or testify, but that's it."

Charlie nodded and exhaled. "Good to know."

"I should have known you were innocent." He shook his head. "I really want to see where we can go without the investigation in the way. I can't seem to get enough of you."

Her resolve melted and her doubtful emotions ebbed. "I kept thinking about you too. I want to not feel anything for you. I know you travel for your work and I'm … I just…"

"Will you go out with me on a real date so we can start over?"

She bit her lip. She wasn't sure if she wanted to risk her heart on another man so soon after her divorce. "Zander, I don't—"

"Look." He held up a finger. "Just think about it, okay?"

Her head nodded before she realized what she wanted.

Zander exhaled and stood. He held out an open palm to her. "Come on."

Her body shivered at the warmth of his rough hand against hers. "Where are we going?"

He opened the door and shut it after her. "I told Pop that I would help him today. The more hands, the better."

"For what?" Noises came from Maria's apartment, the door sat open.

"Maria is moving today."

Charlie should have dropped the charges so Maria wouldn't be alone. She dug her heels into the floorboards. Her heart raced in her chest. Panic coursed through her body. Her forehead got clammy. "I can't help Maria."

"Why?" He stopped and looked at her.

"I'm the one putting her out."

He lifted his eyebrows. "Really?"

She nodded. "It's a long story, but I don't think she wants to see me right now."

"Trust me on this one." He smiled and tugged on their joined hands.

Her body trembled when they entered Maria's door. Everything was catawampus. Tables weren't in the right places, the beautiful ornate rug under her sofa was missing, and the sofa itself was gone. Music played from the radio. Milt looked at her. Corbin smiled and nodded.

She still couldn't digest the connection between Corbin and Zander. She saw the resemblance now. The gold flecks in their eyes. They had the same shoulder span despite Zander's height advantage. Standing next to each other, she saw the same smile on their faces.

Maria stepped out of the kitchen. "There she is!"

Charlie inhaled while Maria approached. The smaller woman seemed different than before. She had a new light in her eyes, something younger. Charlie couldn't find her voice as Maria threw her arms around her for a hug.

"I've been looking for you," Maria said into her ear.

Beth stood at the entrance to the kitchen, hip cocked against the wall, arms folded, and a wide grin.

Speechless, Charlie remained in the hug until Maria stepped back.

"Did you know that the city found my daughter and grandson?"

Charlie swallowed and nodded.

"Of course." Maria glanced at Beth then back. "Beth probably told you everything."

"Not everything, M," Beth said. "She doesn't know why you're moving."

"The place isn't big enough." Maria's smile could warm a glacier. She threw out her arms and giggled. "My grandson's lawyer worked out a deal. He's a good boy so they put him in my custody. He's living with me while he gets counseling once a day. They thought it was a good idea to give him a stable home life and I'll make sure he stays out of trouble. He's also got to do some community service, but..." She shrugged. "He's here."

"What about Dottie?" Charlie's heavy relief spoke before she thought about what she should say. "I mean, the last time I saw her she was unhappy."

"Oh." Maria's voice dropped. But she continued to smile. "Change is hard for everyone. Dottie is required to stay in the recovery center for a while. She has some bigger issues to work out before she's capable of living without care. But, I get to see her whenever I want. We're working through stuff. It'll take a little faith on both our parts. Overall, these are steps in the right direction. I've got a second chance with my family." The light in her eyes sparkled.

"I owe it to you, Charlie. If you hadn't run into them and held them responsible for what they did, I might have never found them again. Dottie and her son would be on the streets still, struggling."

Charlie glanced at Zander and Corbin arguing about how to move the table. Zander looked at her, winked, then went back to work.

"Sometimes the system works," Corbin said. "Way to keep strong."

Charlie knew he was referencing the steakhouse conversation after Beth had mentioned Maria's connection to the alley fight. Corbin had reassured her that the public systems were there to help people when they couldn't see they needed it. A smile emerged on Charlie's lips.

"Charlie?" Maria's serious tone tore Charlie's attention away from the guys. "Kids get into trouble, you know? Sage, my grandson, hasn't had it easy. Can you forgive him so we can still be friends?"

Obvious concern and hope married in Maria's expression. Charlie's anxiety and guilt dissolved. The bumps and bruises had worked out for everyone. Maria, Dottie, and Sage had found each other. Charlie made a new friend in Maria.

Charlie said, "Of course. I'm certain you'll keep him straight."

"As an arrow." Maria gently squeezed Charlie's bicep in a mini-hug and pivoted towards the kitchen. "Now, will you help me move? I know it's a lot to ask. You've already done so much for me, but I've got to get set before the week ends."

"I'd love to help." Charlie followed her into the kitchen.

Chapter 17

The move ended around two in the morning. The group decided to rest at Charlie's after transplanting Maria upstairs into one of the new, bigger apartments. Beth and Corbin lounged on a loveseat that Maria gave Charlie. The loveseat didn't match Charlie's current sofa, but it reminded Charlie of Maria's happy ending.

Zander's head lay in her lap and she enjoyed the feel of his hair between her fingers. The dark strands contrasted her ivory skin.

When he looked at her in the low light, his smile eased the weariness from a busy couple of days. He seemed happier. The way Corbin and he talked made it seem as though they hadn't disconnected at all.

"So." Beth's peppy voice made Charlie smile. Her best friend was a night person. They hadn't talked about the muted tension between them. When the timing was right, they would revisit the awkwardness. This was how they did things.

She continued, "I was going to ask earlier, but we were too busy. What's with the suit, Charlie?"

"I got a new accountant job." Her stomach flipped then flopped, giving into gravity. Her rested heart jolted into a faster beat.

"Yeah?" Beth's pep dipped into concern laced with frustration. "Where?"

She swallowed. "One of my Dad's companies."

"Sounds like congratulations are in order," Zander said.

"No." Beth left Corbin on the sofa and turned off the television. She shifted into the kitchen and flipped on a brighter overhead light. "That's not right. You ditched your father and his influences for this life. I thought you said you wanted to do things on your own." She pointed at the floor. "Why are you giving in now?"

"It's not a big deal." Charlie shrugged at the lie. "My plan didn't work out."

"What do you mean?"

Charlie exhaled when Zander shifted, sitting next to her, concern knitted in the middle of his forehead. He said, "What am I missing? A new job should be a good thing."

"Not in this case." Beth threw her arms out. "Not through her father."

Charlie said, "Let it rest, Beth. I was wrong."

"Wrong?" Beth placed her hands on her hips. "After everything you've been through, you want to go back to where you were? You want to be a servant to your father? Be on his schedule? Have his friends that are only nice to you because you're related?"

"Hey—" Charlie stood.

"Wait." Corbin spread his hands, palms out. "Hold on, this isn't going to end—"

Beth continued, "You left because you've been so lonely in his house. Peter is gone most of the year. There's nobody there for you. He hasn't changed. You want to go back to that?"

When Charlie didn't answer, Beth pressed on. "And what about his job?"

"I went to school for accounting. It's what I do." Charlie couldn't control the lift in her voice. "Years of tuition shouldn't go to waste."

"You said it was mind-numbing."

"I didn't think you understood me."

"Oh, please." She folded her arms. "Charlie, you're not happy doing that job. I saw it through college. The way you hated the homework. You barely passed half your classes. Then you worked for your father, complaining everyday. You did it for Kenneth only because you were married to him. You wanted to do something different. Why go back to it now?"

"I have nothing else to do!" Charlie stood. She glared at Beth. "I'm just as unhappy here as I am there. At least I'll make good money."

Beth stepped forward, not backing down. "How many times do we have to go through this? You don't need the money. You've got millions coming to you next year. Besides, you've said it a thousand times. Money doesn't make you happy."

"Working is better than nothing," Charlie yelled. "It's what I do."

"It's what you have done." Beth lifted her arms. "Look around you. Open your eyes. You've created something here."

She thought about Maria's second chance at being a mother, a grandmother. Charlie glanced at the reunited brothers and her heartbeat skipped. Then Charlie remembered the situation with Milt and the apartment. Zander had mentioned that her letter of recommendation had swayed the building's owner into giving Milt his job back.

Beth said, "You call this nothing?"

Charlie tore her attention away from the men and looked at Beth.

"This is your place. I've never seen you happier than you were before our fight." Beth's voice softened. "I'm sorry about how I handled it. I didn't know what to say. Corbin and I—"

"—are great together." Charlie finished for her. "I'm happy for you."

"Really? You're not mad?" Beth's anger dissolved.

"How can I be? You're my best friend and I only want you to be happy. If I have to give up Corbin, well…" She shrugged.

"Nice to know I meant so much to you," Corbin mumbled.

Zander chuckled.

Charlie's stare met Corbin's playful expression. She said, "Well, you were way too nice for me anyway. I like a challenge."

Zander covered his surprise with a cough.

Corbin placed a hand on his chest, feigning hurt. "Guess I'll get over it. Might take a while, though." He winked. "You are a good kisser."

Zander exploded off the couch and smacked Corbin in the shoulder. "Enough of that!" The men laughed, wrestled a little.

Beth joined in the spirit. "I never want to hear that again either."

"Okay. Okay." Corbin shoved Zander away. "Never again. I promise."

Zander dropped onto the couch. "Glad that's settled. What's next?"

Beth approached Charlie for a hug. Charlie closed her eyes and tenderly accepted her friend. The connection centered her world. Beth, the voice of reason, showed her that she had changed on many levels. Her self-destruction wasn't contagious. She broke the mold. The risk had paid off and she was different.

"Awe, that's sweet." Corbin commented.

Beth eased back, broke contact, and marched to Corbin where she planted a kiss onto his lips. She sat on his lap with a huge smile and Charlie sat next to Zander. He held her hand, smiled.

"We should help Charlie," Beth said.

Charlie lifted her eyebrows in silent question.

Beth continued, "She has this coin." She told them about giving balloons to children the other day in order to cheer them up.

"She showed me the coin too." Corbin nodded. "You still doing that?"

"I ah—" Nervous energy bubbled through Charlie's body.

"So, the coin is real?" Zander exhaled, shook his head, and looked at her. His brown eyes sparkled with new light. "Can I see it?"

"No." Charlie closed her eyes. "I sold it to a coin dealer a couple of days ago."

"What? Why?" Beth straightened in her chair.

"I thought it was another waste of time. I was doing all these things then you all weren't around and Dad said ... I was confused." She admitted.

"And your dad is very convincing." Beth nodded, understanding. "It's too early in the morning to get the coin back. All the businesses are closed right now." Beth puzzled with her lower lip between her teeth. "But what did it say to do last?"

"Doesn't matter. It's not going to happen. Ever." Charlie let go of Zander's hand. She stood. The nervous energy got worse with the memory of what was on the coin. "I can't do it."

"Sure you can. We'll all help." Zander said. "What was it?"

"Bungee jump." Charlie folded her arms and closed her eyes. She lifted her chin to the ceiling, suddenly exhausted. "I'm never doing that."

"Why? I've done it a few times. It's fun." Zander said.

"She has acrophobia." Beth explained. "Pretty bad when we were kids."

"The idea of jumping off anything makes my heart race."

"You can do it." Zander said.

Charlie looked at each of her friends. They were anxious and willing.

Beth said, "We can do it with you."

"Yeah." Corbin put in. "We'll all do it."

Zander's smile had her hedging. She said, "I don't know."

"We should get some sleep. Then, in a few hours, we'll get the coin back and go jumping together." Beth stood, stretched, and pulled on Corbin's hand. "Let's go."

Corbin nodded and followed Beth to the door. "Sounds like fun."

"Bye, guys," Zander said. "See you in a few."

"Will do." Corbin closed the door after them.

"I can't do it." Charlie said to Zander. "And now, I can't sleep."

Zander stood, placed his open hands on either side of her face. He looked into her eyes with a thoughtful attitude. "One thing at a time. Let me help you sleep. We'll worry about the jump when we're there. Okay?"

She opened her mouth and he brushed his lips against hers. She couldn't think about anything else. His masterful tongue danced with hers as he closed the gap between them. She couldn't deny how good his solid, calm body fit hers. She had missed him and she gave into the craving to reconnect.

Chapter 18

Charlie stood in front of Greg Strike. Her mouth fell open at his words. He had sold the coin to someone. He said, "It didn't work anyway."

Her mouth dried and her heart raced at the idea of not getting the coin back. Thinking back, she had made lots of mistakes in the last few days, including giving into her father and taking a job she knew wouldn't make her happy.

But the biggest mistake was selling the coin. It had helped her change her life.

In her sleepless night, she had realized how the empty hole in her chest wasn't as empty anymore. She loved Shadow and intended to retrieve him from her father's home later tonight. She coveted her own place, the privacy, and the freedom. She had made new friends with Zander, Corbin, and Maria.

And she wanted to finish the coin's tasks and see what else it had in store for her.

"You keep records of your sales, right?" Zander wasn't swayed. "Tax purposes."

"Yes, but I can't give that to you. It's personal record."

"Sure you can." Zander showed his badge.

Greg studied the identification and retrieved a book under the glass display case.

This early, the coin shop was empty except for Corbin, Beth, Zander, and Charlie.

"Here it is," Mr. Strike said. "We sold the coin to Peter Davies the day after we got it." He snapped the book shut. "If you want more, you'll have to get a warrant or something."

"Thanks. That's all we needed." Zander rested his arm around Charlie's waist and escorted her out of the store.

She was speechless. What would her father want with the coin she had sold?

"That's good news," Beth said on the way to the car. She fished out her phone and dialed her father's number.

"Hello, thank you for calling Big Tech. This is Mr. Davies's office and I'm Gina Valentino. How may I help you?"

"I'm Mr. Davies's daughter, Charlie, and I would like to speak with him."

"Hi, Charlie, he told me about you," Ms. Valentino said. "I'm sorry, but Mr. Davies is out of town. I can send a message to him if you'd like."

"When will he be back in town?"

"Tomorrow."

"I'd like to schedule lunch with him."

Papers shuffled on the line. "He's not available at that time."

"Where is his lunch meeting taking place?"

"Frankie's Restaurant."

She thanked the efficient assistant and disconnected the call. Charlie intended to crash her father's lunch to talk with him about the coin and why he bought it. She said to the group, "He's out of town today. I'll meet with my father tomorrow and get the coin."

"Great." Beth said. "That frees up our evening. Now let's get going. We have a bungee-jumping appointment to keep."

Charlie's stomach flip-flopped at the idea of bungee-jumping today. Her fear of heights developed when she had fallen from a horse at a young age. The horse had trampled around her and scared her to death. She never forgot the sensation of falling to the ground under the beast. The fear of being out of control iced the hot blood in her veins.

"Maybe we should get breakfast first."

"I packed a picnic." Beth opened the car door and smiled. "We'll eat on the way. It's a long drive."

They climbed into Corbin's four-door sedan. Beth and Corbin in the front seat, Zander and Charlie in the back. She wasn't sure where the relationship was going, but for now, she wouldn't fight fate this time. She interlaced her fingers with Zander's for comfort.

"I'm not sure about this," she whispered.

"The more fears you face, the more you own your life," Zander encouraged.

Charlie looked out the window at zilch. Her mind whirled with past memories of her fear. The times she had stood on hill edges, bridges, or to close to the ledge of balconies. She hadn't minded the brick view through her sliding glass doors in her apartment because it helped her forget she wasn't on the ground floor.

Her heated palms became damp. She inhaled slow and deep for control.

"Everything will be okay. I've done this a few times. It's easier than jumping out of an airplane." Zander said.

She nodded, swallowed nothing from her dry mouth, and couldn't look at him. "How many times have you done this?"

"Not sure." He tenderly squeezed her hand in his. "It's safe. I wouldn't risk your life on anything."

The warm-heartedness in his eyes made her body tremble. She rubbed her thumb on the back of his hand and inhaled her chamomile soap from his skin. She liked the combination.

Despite his failed efforts to calm her down, he had made her night wonderful. He drew her a bath, massaged every muscle in her body, and melted her anger at him for not believing her about the drugs. "Thank you for last night. It was … nice to have someone take care of me."

When he smiled, she realized he had a dimple on the right side of his unshaven face. The dark stubble accentuated the sexy dip. Her eyes studied his full lower lip and her body zinged at the idea of his mouth on hers. She looked away, picked at nothing on her jeans.

He leaned closer. His warm breath caressed her neck. "I could get used to taking care of you, Charlie."

She looked out of the corner of her eye at him. Heat surfaced on her cheeks.

He settled back in the chair and retrieved his phone from his pocket.

"What are you doing?" Charlie asked.

"I'm making sure things at work are good. Going through email."

She couldn't remain quiet. Her circling thoughts made her anxious. "What happened with Lance and his sister?"

Zander blinked up at her then focused his attention on her. "The case is still open. I can't tell you much about it."

"Is Lance in jail?" Her tightened gut knotted at the idea. She had instigated his arrest when she brought the package of drugs to the teashop.

"No, but his sister is still on trial. She's facing prison time for possession, dealing, plus other crimes associated with selling stolen goods."

"Is Lance okay?"

"I haven't seen him. After a case is over, I move on."

"Move on?" The hair on her neck rose. "What do you mean?"

"I'm a undercover agent. I can't work in the same area where my cover is blown. It's too dangerous. I've got to move on until things settle down."

She let his hand go. "So, you're moving?"

"I don't really live anywhere." He lowered his phone, the screen darkened. He rubbed his chin and looked around the car then out the window. "I see more airports than homes."

"Zander." She set her hands in her lap and faced him more. "How do you see us working out?"

He locked stares with her. "I'll find a case that's not far from here. I'll take weekends, days here and there, for visits. I want to stay in touch with my Dad's life. Corbin and I've still got to find our other brother too. He might be in Seattle."

She didn't like the idea of seeing him on a part-time basis. She waved a hand between them. "I thought we were working on something here."

"We are," he said. He placed his palm over hers and rested them on her lap. "The main reason for me to come back here is you."

"I can't do it that way." She looked at his thick fingers. She realized the next things she said might break their relationship before it started. "My ex-husband traveled for work. It wasn't a good experience."

"I'm not your ex-husband." His flat tone pulled her stare from their hands. "I don't care what he did. You've got to make the distinction and you've got to trust me. I won't cheat on you. I'm not that way."

Surprise opened her eyes wide. "How do you know—?"

"I studied your file, remember?" He looked away. "I know what that jackass did to you and why you divorced."

She covered his trembling hand with her free one wanting to ease his anger. "It's not you. I know you're nothing like Kenneth. He never connected with me like you have. I just don't want that kind of relationship again. The traveling. I want someone home, at my table, in my life, every day."

She looked him in the eyes again. She blinked with her building disappointment. Her heart ached. "I'm tired of being lonely."

"Me too," Zander whispered. "I put in for—"

"I've got sandwiches. Who wants ham on rye?"

Zander said, "Beth, as usual, your timing is impeccable."

Charlie couldn't help the small smile as she reached for the sandwich.

"Roast beef and cheddar?" Beth wasn't fazed by Zander's words.

"I'll take that one." Corbin snagged the food from Beth's hand.

"Hey," Zander complained.

"I've got two of those." Beth handed Zander another sandwich and a couple of cans. "Sodas?"

. . .

"Here we are!" Beth said from the front seat. The conversation had jumped from one person to the next in the car. Charlie couldn't get another personal word in with Zander. But she didn't mind too much. She needed to believe in the relationship right now.

Beth cheered, "I'm so excited. I've never done this before and I've always wanted to do it. Come on."

Beth was out of the car first followed by Corbin and Zander, but Charlie couldn't bring herself to open the door.

Zander circled the car then opened her door. He held out an open palm. "Come on. Face your fears. It's hard to do for everyone but you'll be happy you did this. We'll take it step by step."

She hedged out of the car. "Why am I doing this?"

"You're brave and you don't let anything limit your life." Zander put his arm around her while they walked. "Besides, it's a big turn-on."

She lifted her eyebrows at him. "Really?"

"Hell yeah." He chuckled. His wide smile encouraged her footsteps. "I like a woman who can take control of things. She's got a strong head on her shoulders."

A smile emerged on Charlie's lips. She joined the waiting group at the trailhead. Beth tugged at Corbin's arm. "Come on."

He laughed. "This is why I love you. You're not afraid of anything."

Charlie pressed her lips. He'd find out soon enough that Beth had fears.

The trail was lined with enormous Douglas fir, western hemlock, and western red cedar trees. The old forest had a comfortable, closed-in feel. A thick canopy of growth covered most of the sky from view. A cool breeze randomly tickled Charlie's skin and the leaves rustled. She held Zander's hand leading to the bungee bridge.

Dread mounted with each step.

Through the trees, she spotted a sparkling river and her heart hammered. Her quick breathing was due to the walk, not the fear of falling off a bridge with a small rope tied around her waist.

She shook her head, looked at her sneaker covered feet, and concentrated on one foot in front of the other.

Zander's confident steps encouraged her without words. Zander squeezed her hand and chatted with Corbin while Beth led the way. Charlie barely caught the name *Decker* in her self-absorbed fog.

She saw the bridge's edge-clearing front of them and stumbled. Handrails were attached to metal poles on the side of the mountain. She couldn't catch her breath. She planted her heels into the ground. "Oh, crap, what am I doing? This is crazy."

Tears formed in her eyes. She shook.

"I'll catch up to Beth and get this party started." Corbin jogged ahead.

"Look at me." Zander commanded. "Charlie, look at me."

She did and her mind settled a little at the sight of gold flecks highlighted in his brown eyes from the sun in the clearing. Those sinfully long dark lashes helped to mesmerize her. "You can do this. We both know it."

She closed her eyes and inhaled. She thought about how she overcame singing in public, one of her worst fears ever, and she could do this too. Despite the panic in her belly, she nodded. She opened her eyes. "Okay."

His smile stretched from ear to ear. He inched toward the bridge walking backwards. "There's my woman."

In a weird, primitive way, she liked the sound of that. She followed his lead, ignored the mounting acid in her stomach at the approaching challenge. "Don't say that again."

He laughed. "My woman."

She shoved his shoulder playfully.

"One day, I'll hear you say 'my man' and all will be good in the world." He guided her toward the platform while her mind puzzled on Zander's statement. Could they make it work? Could he be content with just her? Would he cheat like Kenneth?

No. She trusted him. What he said in the car was right. He wasn't Kenneth. Kenneth was insincere and self absorbed. She didn't see any of that in Zander.

Her foot landed on a cement slab and her knees weakened. She glanced around at the open-aired river crossing. A huge apparatus sat in the center of the bridge. People grouped around a couple of tables under white awnings. Beth and Corbin hunched over one of the tables with pens in their hands, signing waivers.

"I can't do this." Her voice cracked.

"It's already done," Zander said. "You're here. Let's go."

She shook her head, but her feet continued onto the walkway. "What if something goes wrong? What if I die?"

"Think about this." Zander eased backwards. "This company wouldn't be here if people died because of the experience. They've been in business for many years."

She nodded. "Makes sense. Dead people equal bad business."

"Damn right." He lifted a clipboard with papers on it. "Now, just sign these papers. Don't read them. I've already looked at them. It's all okay."

She scribbled her signature. When she looked in the near distance, she saw Beth tied into a harness with a huge yellow thing attached. Beth smiled, waved, and fell backward off a platform. The workers stood at the edge, watching her descend. Corbin leaned over the handrail, cheering.

Charlie's heart hammered. She screamed, "Beth! Oh my god, Beth!"

"She's okay." Corbin said and clapped. "Great jump, babe!"

Charlie couldn't catch her breath. "This is so crazy. I can't do it."

"Beth is fine. She's on her way up now." Zander didn't let Charlie go far from him. He held her in his open arm while she stood far from the edge. Beth appeared at the ledge she had fallen from, her hair tussled, and the workers smiled while helping her back onto her feet. They unhooked her.

Beth's cheeks were pink. She ran into Corbin's arms grinning from ear to ear. He lifted her and twirled in a circle. She yelled, "That was a blast. Unbelievable. I want to do it again and again."

Corbin set her on her feet. "My turn."

Beth hugged Charlie, and the sensation settled Charlie's anxiety for her friend's life. She was alive, in her arms, and smiling. The experience wasn't bad.

Charlie couldn't believe how fast the workers had Corbin locked in. He dove like a swimmer off the diving board above a huge pool, not the narrow river below.

Zander laughed out loud and cheered his brother on. Charlie took a few steps back. Beth yelled down to Corbin, "Great dive, honey!"

Charlie turned. Zander caught her and turned her into his arms for a hug. "It's okay, sweetheart. You trust me, right?"

She nodded despite the images of her broken bones splayed across river rock playing in her mind. "I … I guess."

Beth put her arms around Charlie as Zander geared up in a harness. He continued to reassure her that he was fine. He walked her through the process, explaining the safety behind the apparatus. Then he was gone. He fell off the platform.

Her heart hammered, tears formed in her eyes.

His excited yell came on the wind that smacked into her ears.

"Okay, Charlie, your turn." Beth escorted her toward the workers.

"Beth, I'm scared."

"It'll be okay, honey. Look. We're all fine. This is safe."

Charlie couldn't move while they suited her up. She was sure the workers were friendly because Beth and Corbin laughed at what they were saying. Unfortunately, she couldn't make heads or tails of it all. She just kept thinking about what Zander had said about the business. Dead people didn't make a good business.

Zander reappeared on the platform. His cheeks as red as Beth's and his smile as wide. His dark hair messed on his head. He exhaled a laugh. "That was fun."

As he was unhooked, he held out his open arms to her then hugged her close. His body cool against hers, he whispered, "It's so much fun. The three of us did it without an injury. You're going to do fine too. Try to enjoy it."

She couldn't find her voice through her fear. She nodded.

Her legs shook as she stepped up to a wide ledge. She gripped the handrails. Fear choked her throat at the distant view of clouds and forest and … nothing.

"Okay, you've got to let go now." A stranger said in her ear in a matter-of-fact tone. "You can jump whenever you're ready."

"Shit," she whispered. She thought about Corbin diving into a pool and looked back at the group. Zander gestured with a thumbs-up. Corbin spread his hands in a forward-nudging movement, and Beth nodded. She yelled, "The fee is non-refundable. There's no going back now. Seize the moment."

"You people are crazy." Charlie exhaled. Beth knew she would hate the idea of wasting money. With affection, Charlie whispered, "Bitch."

She forced her fingers free from the railing and stepped forward onto a short platform over the abyss. Cool wind lifted her hair from her neck, chilled her skin. Horror bubbled in her chest, causing her doubts to zing around in her thoughts. Pride jumped forward in her mind, making her functional and focused.

She couldn't stand on the edge of the platform only to turn around and give in to her terror. Her newfound self-reliance wouldn't stand for it.

"Okay," the matter-of-fact voice said from over her shoulder. "I'll count down from three…"

"Shit. Shit. Shit." Her muscles trembled. Tears escaped her eyes. Her breath caught somewhere in her body. Dizzy, she closed her eyes. "I can do this."

"…two…"

What would her father think about her on this ledge?

"…three…"

Without another thought, she stepped onto nothing. Time stopped. She opened her eyes and a surreal peace overcame her. She floated in a blur of color. She was flying. No gravity. No thought. No worries. *Light … light…*

Then sensations boomed through her system. Weight. Gravity. The harnesses tightened around her body. Water enveloped her vision, her breathing restarted, and she screamed. Her cheeks were soaked with tears. A tingling sensation tickled along her skin as her blood raced through her veins.

Then she dangled, safely held by the strong cord.

From deep in her chest, a laugh burst into her throat and echoed off the ravine.

"You did it!"

"Great job!"

"I'm so proud of you, sweetheart!"

A small applause hit her eardrums.

She smiled. "I can't believe I did it."

The next thing she knew, the workers on the platform were grabbing her, guiding her to her feet. She couldn't get beyond the thoughts of her experience while they worked to unhook the harness.

When she was free, she forced the muscles in her legs to engage and threw her arms wide for a group hug. Zander, Corbin, and Beth huddled around her. She yelled through a new rush of tears, "I love you guys. I really do!"

Chapter 19

Charlie stepped off the bus into a construction-dominated Seattle. She had gotten the address of the restaurant for her father's lunch appointment.

She had woken up this morning in Zander's arms, a new woman ready to take on anything. Nothing could stop her today.

In her new mental state, she loved her apartment and everything that went with it. She accepted her life, full of challenges, and all. It was her life. She realized that she could focus on the crap or she could focus on the good. It was a matter of perspective. That's why money didn't make people happy, why it didn't make her happy. People made themselves happy simply by point of view, what they saw in their lives. What she saw in *her* life.

She now understood the glass half-empty-or-half-full metaphor.

The bus chugged away, leaving a cloud of pollutants in her lungs. Seattle was different from Bellevue. Seattle was more of a disorganized city with homeless problems and disgruntled city workers with pessimistic attitudes. Bellevue was full of people who smiled and picked up after themselves because they had hometown pride.

Didn't matter. She wouldn't be here long.

The light switched and Charlie marched across the uneven pavement, through the opening in the gates, and onto the docks. Her flats clacked on the wood planks. With its unobstructed views, Frankie's was one of Seattle's more popular waterfront restaurants.

Charlie spotted her father right away. He always sat at the farthest table from the restaurant, wanting the privacy and pretending he owned the view while he entertained some business associate. Part of her hated the idea of interrupting a possible venture, but he had bought her coin for a reason.

After thinking on it, she figured he would use it for leverage. He wanted her to do something. Time to find out what it was.

He looked up, straightened in the chair, and lifted his dark eyebrows in surprise while she approached the table. His associate had his back towards her. She stopped next to the table. "Hi, Dad."

His smile wavered. "Hey, this is a surprise."

"I need to speak with you and it can't wait."

"Well." The voice of his associate intruded on her greeting. She felt an unexpected thump in her chest.

Her attention darted over her ex-husband's body. He looked good in his suit and tie. Not a strand of his dark hair was out of place on his head. His bright white teeth flashed in the partial sunlight.

He said, "We were just talking about you."

"Were you?" she asked flatly.

"Here, have a seat. Gina told me you had called." Peter eased a chair out for her.

She sat with her hands in her lap. Seagulls flew in the distance, their cries echoed in the fouled air. Her throat closed and her lungs constricted. She forced a breath. Seeing Kenneth again made her stomach clench with subdued anger. The last time she had talked with him, he tried to bully her into going back to work for him.

"Peter said you advised him to go ahead with the Ghostlight project." His smile widened more. "Thank you for that."

She didn't want to engage in conversation with Kenneth. She turned to her father and rotated her shoulders away from the cheating bastard. "I came to talk with you about that coin I sold a few days ago."

Peter leaned back in the chair. "You found out I bought it."

She nodded. "I'd like to have it back."

Kenneth chuckled. "When Peter told me about the coin, I knew you didn't want to let it go. We went back together to get it."

She cringed, closed her eyes, and inhaled. "Of course."

"I told you this wasn't over," Kenneth said, gloating.

Charlie opened her eyes and scowled at her father. "Why?"

"You're not acting right." Peter folded his arms. His lightly tanned skin reflected in a sunbeam and he squinted his eyes at her. His pristine suit wrinkled at the shoulders. He sighed. "You won't move back into my house when it's rent-free. The way you treated Beth the other night isn't you. The way you treated me." He shook his head and waved a hand. "You've lost control of everything. I didn't know what to do. I asked Kenneth for advice."

"Kenneth?" She lifted her eyebrows. "Why him?"

"He's the only other one who has lived with you since you left home." Peter rested his elbows on the table. "I figured he could help me."

She exhaled and looked at Kenneth. "You've got the coin."

He tapped his chest pocket. "Keep it with me at all times."

She crossed her legs, folded her arms, and ground her molars. Careful to keep her tone low, she asked, "What do you want?"

"You back at your desk. That's all."

Silence landed between them. The waitress approached the table with a tray full of drinks. The younger woman smiled at Charlie while she served the men. She said to Charlie, "Hello, can I bring you a drink?"

When the woman leaned toward Kenneth, Charlie bumped the tray. Liquid poured over Kenneth and he jumped back. "What the hell?" He yelled. "You incompetent little bitch. How clumsy."

"I'm sorry, sir." The distraught waitress blundered through the chaos.

Charlie grabbed a napkin, helped to wipe Kenneth off, and smiled when he announced that he needed to go to the bathroom to finish cleaning up. Charlie said to the waitress, "It's okay. Don't worry about it."

"Accidents happen," Peter agreed. "He'll settle down. Give us a few minutes."

"I'm so sorry." The waitress frowned and nodded, then hurried off.

People at the surrounding tables reconnected with each other and Charlie faced her father. "I can't believe you let him manipulate you because of this."

"You've always been a good girl, but now, you're out of control—"

"Stop." Charlie held up a hand. "Just stop with the concern bit. Let's be honest here. For the first time, I've made my decisions despite your wants. I don't follow your schedule. That's what's really bothering you."

He huffed.

She rested her hand over his on the table. "Dad, you raised me to be strong. You encouraged me to have my own mind, my own dreams. You've given me the money to live free. I don't even have to work. I really appreciate what you've done. More now than I ever have. But you can't shut me down when I start living those dreams. I've found where I want to be, who I want to become, and that's all that's happened here."

"I can't believe that tart." Kenneth's agitated voice raked on Charlie's nerves. He sat in the chair and complained about his ruined suit. "Unbelievable."

Charlie stood. She looked at Kenneth. "Goodbye."

His eyes widened. "Wait … what?"

She looked at Peter. "Dad, you know where to reach me when you're ready to be a part of my life. I'll be waiting. I love you."

Kenneth grabbed her forearm. "Not so fast."

"Let her go." The threat in Peter's voice scared her and she glanced back at her father. "Or so help me, I will have you arrested."

Kenneth jerked his hand back as if her skin shocked him.

"I've made a huge mistake." Peter stood, dropped his napkin on the table, and leaned closer to Kenneth. "We're done here."

"Peter?" Kenneth blubbered. "What are you talking about?"

"Let this whole thing go or I will be forced to do something you'll regret."

Kenneth sat straighter in his chair. "Like what?"

"Pull my million out of the Ghostlight Project, of course." Peter offered a got-you grin before he placed his hand on Charlie's lower back to escort her out of the restaurant. On the way out of the gated area, he said, "I'm sorry."

She smiled. "Me too."

On the dock, he said, "I'm glad I listened to you about that project or I don't think Kenneth would be sitting there like a nice little boy right now. I'm really sorry about the coin, though."

"Don't be." She lifted her hand, opened her palm, and the coin sparkled in the sunlight. "I've learned a few new tricks these past few weeks. This one came from a friend of mine named Corbin. He taught it to me on my way back from bungee-jumping."

Peter laughed. "You bungee-jumped? Oh, now, there's a story I need to hear. We've got a lot of catching up to do, sweetheart."

…

Zander waited for Charlie at a coffee shop off Fourth Street in Bellevue. He had wanted to go with her to get the coin back from her father, but she had insisted she do it alone.

He learned earlier that day that his request for a year off was approved. He couldn't wait to tell Charlie. At least, they had a year to explore the possibility of a future together. He liked the idea. No, he loved the idea.

Charlie entered the busy coffee house and his breath caught. She had her hair tied in a bun. The dress she wore hugged her curves well. A fresh, pink blush on her cheeks complimented the wide smile on her lips. She slid into the chair across from him. "Sorry I'm late. I had a wonderful afternoon with Dad."

"I'm glad to hear it." He took her hand into his, needing the contact.

She told him what happened at Frankie's

"I can't believe that jackass." He rubbed his chin in an act to calm his tension.

"It's over." She placed his hand between hers. "He has nothing on me anymore, thanks to Corbin teaching me how to pick a pocket."

Zander smiled. There was a moment of silence. "Since we're here, do you want a cup of coffee before we start our date?"

"Look, Zander, I've already been through a bunch of shit when it comes to relationships. Please don't play with me. I'm looking for something real."

He exhaled. "We *are* real."

She folded her arms.

He speared his fingers though his hair.

"What do you want, Zander?"

"Let's just see where this goes tonight, okay?"

She looked everywhere but at him, thinking. Her features softened and she finally said, "I'm going to get a white hot chocolate. Do you want anything?"

He exhaled his relief. He wanted to kiss her right then, so beautiful. Instead, he rubbed his lips with the palm of his hand before he answered. "I'm okay. Thanks."

He watched her enter the line.

She fished something out of her pocket. It looked like a gold coin and she played with it between her fingers. Curious, he continued to watch her. She ordered and paid for the customer behind her in line.

He liked the way she smiled. Her easy demeanor wasn't lost on others. She was definitely impressionable. The man gave her his card. When she returned to the table, she settled in the chair. Her dark eyebrows drew together. "What's wrong? You look really mad."

"Did that guy just give you his phone number?" His shoulder ached.

"Wow! I didn't peg you for the jealous type." She laughed.

He glowered. "Neither did I."

She stroked his hand with her fingers, easing his stress. "Turns out that I've met the guy before because of the coin."

"What do you mean?" He looked at the gold in her hand.

"The first time I met him, his wife was pregnant. We were on a crowded bus and I gave my seat to them. He remembered because he was worried about his wife. She's close to having the child and she was supposed to be on bed rest for the last of her pregnancy. He couldn't say no when she wanted to go to the park."

Zander looked at the excitement in her eyes, the thrill of discovery. Much like the look on her face after she had jumped off the bridge. In empathy, his pulse quickened. "What about this time?"

"He lost his job yesterday. Turns out that he's a construction man. I asked him for his card because Milt is working on the building's fourth level. Thought I'd pass it on." She tucked the card in her jacket pocket.

"So, how does the coin work?"

She handed it to him. "Corbin thought it was a trick, but I'm not a magician. I can't explain how it works. It just does. Here, I'll show you. Look at the words inscribed on the back."

"PAY FOR NEXT IN LINE. Twelve of twenty-one." He lifted his eyebrows in surprise. "Interesting. That's why you caught the attention of the guy behind you."

"I don't think it's a coincidence. I believe there are twenty-one flips to each holder or cycle. Now watch closely." He didn't understand, but she took the coin from him and tossed it.

End over end, the coin spun for what seemed like minutes. The gold sparkled despite cloud cover through the windows and low light in the shop. It seemed to hover in the air briefly. Then it landed in her palm. She closed her fingers around it and inhaled.

Her lips drew into a smile. She handed it back.

Zander frowned. He blinked. "It's a beautiful coin."

"I love the sparkle, happens every time I flip it." Her smile was contagious. "What does it say now?"

He couldn't believe the evidence. He had given her the coin. She hadn't dropped her hands below the table or done any weird waving like a magician would. It was inscribed with one set of words, now it had a different set of words. He couldn't contain his bewilderment. "ADDRESS A WAITER BY NAME. Thirteen of twenty-one."

Her cheeks splotched with red. "See?"

He nodded and handed the coin back to her. The images of her tossing it replayed in his head. He was dead certain she hadn't played a trick. Of course she hadn't. Hadn't he learned that she didn't have a deceptive bone in her body?

She looked at the words too. "Ready to go to dinner?"

Chapter 20

Charlie stood on the balcony of her apartment with the coin in her hand. She had enjoyed the date with Zander last night. She had addressed the waiter by name as soon as they were settled at the table and they had gotten their meal for half price. When the bill came, she flipped the coin again. They did LEAVE A BIG TIP for the waiter, flip 14/21.

Jase Miller, the waiter, had thanked them on the way out of the restaurant by telling them that he needed the money to pay for his next semester at college. He was an intern at the hospital about to lose his placement because he didn't have the tuition.

She smiled at the memory.

It felt good inside to help others. She remembered when she had started in the apartment. She had been freshly divorced and devoid of feeling. Now, things were different. She was different. The coin had helped her change.

She flipped the coin and it sparkled in the sunrise. Her breath caught. It was the most stunning thing she had ever seen. It was magical, all right. Nothing could be that beautiful and not be enchanted. The coin warmed her hand when it landed in her palm.

New words were etched on the backside and her eyebrows pulled together with the puzzle.

"Hey, sweetheart, what are you doing out here?" Zander stepped onto the deck, barefooted, dressed in sweats and a t-shirt. He gave her a tender hug, kissed her neck, and held her close. "I love that you're not afraid of heights anymore."

"It feels good."

He told her about his year of leave. She wasn't certain what would happen after his time was up. In a strange way, her anxiety mounted at the possibility of losing him to his work, but he was worth the risk.

"I just flipped the coin again. Look what it says."

"GIVE A SECOND CHANCE. Fifteen of twenty-one." He read the coin from her open palm. "What do you suppose that means?"

"I'm not sure."

"Come on inside. I made breakfast." He held her hand while they walked through the door and to the table. He pulled out a chair for her. She settled, and admired the eggs, bacon, and potatoes on the nicely set table. Guilt and admiration clawed at her insides.

"Does it bother you that I don't cook?"

"Not when I can." He sat next to her and placed a napkin on his leg. "Does it bother you?"

"Yes." She worried her lower lip. "I'd like to learn."

"I'd be happy to teach you." He winked.

She giggled. "Something tells me it will take a long time to get through one lesson with you."

"Does that bother you?" He served her eggs.

"Not at all." She picked up her fork and dug into the food. After she ate half her plate, she wondered about the words on the coin. "It's never been so vague before."

"Maybe it's not being vague. Don't think so hard. How would you accomplish the task, just say off the top of your head?" He set his fork down and drank coffee from the mug in front of him. The words SOME DAYS JUST AREN'T WORTH PUTTING ON A BRA stared back at her.

"I've got it." She exploded out of the chair and ran into the bedroom in search of her jogging gear where she left the card. "I've got to find it."

Zander stood in the doorway drinking his coffee. "Find what?"

"The plowman's card."

"The what?"

She smiled when she fished it out of her inner jogging coat pocket. "Walla! He gave it to me the day he picked up his shovels when the store closed."

Zander didn't appear impressed. He leaned a casual hip against the wall.

"This is it." She read the name and number on the card then lifted her phone from the dresser. Her fingers quickly dialed. "I've got to organize a second chance for the communities consignment store."

The plowman picked up on the third ring. "Carl here. What can I do for ya?"

Three hours later, Charlie opened her apartment door for Carl. He brought a friend with him and introduced them. Carl had a charming smile on his slim face. The middle-aged man was taller than she remembered. He said, "I'm so happy you're doing this. I don't know why I didn't think of it myself. It makes sense."

"I'm just glad you're willing to help with it on such short notice. I don't think I can pull this off without everyone on board." Charlie closed the door.

Her apartment was packed with people. She had called everyone she recently met to the meeting. Corbin, Zander, and Milt were talking with Juan Rodriguez in the kitchen. Juan was the pregnant woman's husband, the one who needed a contracting job. It looked like Milt and he were getting along well. Maybe Juan would have a job by the end of the day. The thought made Charlie smile.

Carl and his new friend found Maria on the couch and started a conversation. Charlie didn't know Maria and Carl were friends. From the way they spoke, they hadn't seen each other for a while.

A knock came at the door again.

Charlie answered and greeted her father. He brought Steve, the aged butler, with him to the meeting. Charlie said, "I'm glad you want to be a part of this, Dad."

"I'm glad you let me after what I tried to do." He dropped his chin to his chest and a blush painted bright on his high cheekbones. "The more I think about what you said, the more I believe you were right the entire time. I didn't want you to leave home."

"Let's move forward and make some new memories. Okay?"

"Hi, Charlie." Suzie Walker, the new assistant superintendent, came up behind Peter and Steve at the door. Her blonde hair was piled on her head in a messy bun and she hugged a clipboard to her chest. "I'm a little late. It couldn't be helped. Have I missed anything?"

"I'm about to start. Come in and find a spot. I don't have much space in the apartment, but it'll work for what we need today." Charlie stepped back, allowing the three into her home. She closed the door and took a moment to enjoy the gathering. She had read somewhere that people get so caught up in striving for a perfect life that they forgot to slow down and relish moments like this. In this moment, she wasn't alone. She had a wonderful group of new friends. Each person helped to fill her life with challenge, joy, and purpose.

She twirled the coin between her fingers and frowned. She had called Lance, wanting to talk with him about what had happened between them and see if they could work it out. He didn't answer his phone or return her calls.

Her stomach turned with added guilt for getting him and Lily arrested.

"Okay, everyone," Charlie said. She exhaled and put her troubled thoughts to rest in the back of her mind. She tucked the coin in her pocket and looked at everyone. "First off, thanks for coming on short notice. I really appreciate you helping me out with this."

She waited for the group to quiet down and all eyes were on her. "I'm sure you're all wondering what this is about. Sorry I couldn't tell you more when I called you. I wanted to explain with everyone in the room.

"I have a friend and her name is Rebecca Jordan. She runs a small corner consignment shop a few blocks from here."

Charlie pointed at Carl. "My friend Carl knows Rebecca. He's been selling his items in her shop for years."

"They're really good people," Carl added.

"Unfortunately, Rebecca had financial trouble and she closed the shop. Carl's informed me that, without Rebecca's shop, the contributing community is suffering. I really want to help my new friend and my local community. It's going to take a lot of hard work in a short time. I can't do it myself.

"I'm asking for a favor from all of you. We all come from different lives, know different people." She fished out her phone and held it up for the group to see. "If everyone here takes fifteen minutes to spread the word to their contacts, we can surprise Rebecca with a grand reopening like no other."

"What if she doesn't want the shop?" Beth asked.

Carl spoke up. "She does. She loves that shop."

"I haven't spoken with her in a while, but I know that shop was Rebecca's dream." Maria contributed. "I'll do anything I can to help reopen it."

Peter stepped forward. "I hate to be the bad-news guy. If we do all the work to reopen the shop, it sounds like she won't have the finances to keep it open. We might be adding a burden more than helping her out."

"This is the brilliant part, thanks to Charlie." Carl threw his hands wide. "With everyone getting together to make this big, we can bring in more people, more money, than the shop normally draws in a year. We can rebuild her reserves and it's like she gets to start over."

Juan asked, "Why did she lose all the money in the first place? Is she irresponsible?"

"Far from it. The shop has been open for a long time now. Rebecca knows how to pinch a penny, believe me." Carl shook his head, his expression turned grim. "Her husband has been in the hospital for almost a year recovering from a accident. Rebecca had to use her reserve money for his care. He leaves the hospital this Friday, but he won't be able to work the same job."

Juan nodded in understanding, as did a few others in the room.

"Rebecca's life is that shop and without her husband getting a paycheck, they won't be able to qualify for a loan even if they tried." Carl said. "We all know it takes years to recover that kind of money under the best circumstances."

Murmurs drifted through the group.

Charlie said, "Our efforts could really give Rebecca and our local community a boost. It won't take much to get everyone you know to the store. This is an opportunity to give something. To help out where it really counts."

"I'm in." Zander stepped forward. "How is this going to work?"

Chapter 21

Charlie hustled into the kitchen and opened a can of cat food for Shadow. Her hands shook with nervous energy. Over the past week, she worked hard at organizing the grand reopening of Jordan's Corner store. Suzie offered to assist where she could and Charlie was grateful. She didn't realize how much time it took to plan such a big event.

Charlie called for the cat.

Suzie had convinced her grandfather to change the pet policy in the building. Shadow was now, legally, welcome in Charlie's home. Peter had dropped the cat off before he left town yesterday morning. He intended to return in time for the grand reopening today.

Fresh fish wafted in the small kitchen from the can. Shadow jumped onto the counter. Charlie stroked the cat's soft hair and left him to eat.

She couldn't stand still for very long. Excitement spun in her system. The Jordans didn't know about the reopening. Carl said he and the community wanted to make it a surprise for when they returned from the hospital for the last time.

Charlie looked at her watch and lifted her voice. "You ready to go?"

Juan stepped out of the bedroom dressed in jeans and a button-down shirt that matched his brown eyes. His wet, dark hair was slicked back from his face. He stood about her height and weight. "Yes," he said in a thick Spanish accent. "Thank you for letting me use your bathroom."

"I couldn't have you going to the reopening covered in sawdust." She smiled. "Thanks for helping me get people there. I love your family. They helped out so much."

"No problem. We are happy to be part of it." He followed her to the door. "And did I say thanks for getting me the construction work from Mr. Green."

"Only a few times." She laughed and locked the door behind her. "Let's get going. We're a little late now." She hurried down the stairs, out the building, and on the street.

The sun shone in full glory. She lifted her hand over her eyes, looking for the bus. "Come on. Let's catch this one."

She started to run, Juan at her side. Then Juan pulled up short. Charlie stopped too. The bus eased up to the curb across the street and half a block away.

"My wife." Juan's voice cracked. "She's in labor."

"Wait, what?" Charlie's heart raced in her chest. She focused on Juan. "She's having the baby right now? Where?"

"She's at the house. She's worried something is wrong." He looked at her with worry written all over his face. "I've got to go to her."

"Where do you live?" She fished out her phone.

Juan started running in the opposite direction from the bus. Charlie followed him. He said, "Not far from here. We can get there faster by running."

Charlie nodded. She held her phone in her hand, unable to make a call.

Juan held a brisk pace for five blocks and turned into a yard. The house was old, with overgrowth in front. Boards covered the windows and Juan shoved open a door with a hole in the middle. He called, "Amy!"

A woman screeched from the back of the house.

Charlie's adrenaline pumped. She followed Juan down the tattered hall. In the kitchen, a woman was on the floor. She had her back resting against worn, white cabinets. So young.

Juan fell to his knees next to the woman. "Amy," he continued in Spanish.

Amy said something back.

"I don't speak Spanish. What are you saying?" Charlie said.

"She's in lots of pain. She's swearing at me." He held her hand and kissed her knuckles then he snaked his arm around her upper back. "Let's get you to the hospital."

Amy shook her head. "We can't afford a hospital."

"The family is at the reopening." Juan argued. "I don't know how to deliver this baby. We need to go to the hospital."

"If you had paid attention when—" Amy screeched and grabbed her belly. Her English faded to Spanish and her face scrunched in pain.

Charlie hurried to help Juan lift his pregnant wife off the floor. The struggle strained every muscle in Charlie's body. She held tight to the phone while they worked together, moving toward the hallway.

"No!" Amy fell to the floor with a miserable shout. Water from Amy spread under them.

Juan moved fast and caught his wife's head before it knocked against the floor.

Amy screamed again, something in Spanish.

Charlie's feet slipped, she didn't let go of Amy's arm, and landed on her knees next to the woman. "What did she say?"

"She's not going to make it to the hospital." Juan's voice cracked again.

Charlie let Amy go and dialed 911. She handed the phone to Juan, knowing the operator needed the address. "Don't worry about the bill. Just get us some help."

"This is not our house." Amy's voice dropped to a malevolent tone.

Charlie wrapped her arm around Amy's shoulders. "We'll work it out. We need help right now."

Juan nodded. He spoke to the operator, answering questions.

Amy's body trembled and she bawled.

Charlie supported Amy as much as she could. "It's going to be okay."

Amy's face contorted, she tensed and dropped her head back. The high-pitched scream hurt Charlie's ears, unsettled her calm.

Charlie said, "Deep breaths. Come on, Amy, take deep breaths with me."

Amy's green eyes focused on Charlie. She nodded and inhaled.

"Good," Charlie praised. "How old are you?"

"Twenty," Amy said through clenched teeth. "We can't afford…" Another wail tore from her throat and Charlie held onto the shaking woman.

Juan dropped the phone to grab hold of Amy when she arched backward. "Help is on the way. I'm going to grab some pillows and towels. I'll be right back. Okay?"

Amy righted herself. "Hurry."

Charlie tried again to clam her. "We met on the bus a while back. Do you remember?"

Amy nodded, breathed. "You helped Juan find a job."

Juan returned and placed pillows under Amy's back. He swiped at the water on the floor and stretched out some new towels around his wife. The dress Amy wore was soaked to her waist, but covered most of her legs.

Sirens sounded outside. Juan jumped to his feet and rushed to the door. Some of the tension in Charlie's shoulders drained. "Help is here."

Amy cried.

Juan returned with three men dressed in EMT uniforms. He spoke in rapid Spanish to one of them who nodded. The man squatted and made eye contact with Charlie. He said, "It's you."

Charlie smiled. "It's good to see you. Have you delivered a baby before?"

"Thanks to you, I took a class on it a couple of days ago." He chuckled.

Amy shrieked, drawing their attention.

"Okay," The medic said. "Deep breaths. What's your name?"

"Amy," Charlie answered. "Her name is Amy."

"My name is Jase Miller." He nodded. "I'm here to help. We're going to do this together. Okay?"

...

Charlie waved to the ambulance when it drove away. She stood, stunned, for a moment, the miracle of birth fresh on her mind. She had witnessed something unique. How did people do it? How did they go from one amazing experience back to reality?

Reality.

She looked at her watch and remembered the Jordan's reopening. Thank goodness, Carl had the keys. Suzie knew the planned routine. The party could happen without her.

Charlie glanced at her clothes. They were coated in gunk and blood. She needed to run home to change. Luckily, her adrenaline hadn't crashed and she used it to run back the way Juan had brought her to the house. It didn't take long for her to enter her apartment's front gate.

Almost everyone in the building was attending the reopening. She rushed up the stairs and into her apartment. Zander came out of the bedroom, then looked at her from head to toe. "What in the hell happened to you?"

"Juan's wife had her baby. I helped." Charlie hurried past Zander. She tore off her shirt and started unbuttoning her pants. Her hands shook. It took her a second to maneuver the button from the hole. "I want a quick shower."

"What was it?" Zander stood in the doorway of the bathroom.

She turned on the water, stripped the rest of the way, and stepped under the spray. He had said something. She jerked her head out of the spray then asked. "What?"

"The baby," Zander folded his arms and rested a shoulder against the doorframe. "Was it a boy or girl?"

"Boy." Charlie rushed the shower, turned off the water, and grabbed a towel. She shifted past Zander again to grab clothes from her dresser. "It was amazing. I still can't wrap my head around what just happened. Juan went to the hospital with the baby and his wife. He asked me to deliver the news to his family when I arrived at the shop."

She dragged a comb through her hair. "Did I miss Rebecca's arrival from the hospital with her husband?"

"I'm not sure. I got worried and borrowed Corbin's car to come get you."

"Thanks." She kissed him on the cheek then switched her wallet, phone, and keys, to the pockets in her clean jeans. "Ready?"

"Wait." He hooked an arm around her drawing her into a hug. "You're amazing, you know that?"

She took the moment in, the warmth of his body and masculine scent of his skin at his neck. It eased her nervous energy. She loved the way he fit. She turned her head to his ear and whispered, "I think I love you."

He inched back. His eyes considered her features from her forehead to mouth.

"I just thought you should know." She stepped out of his arms and hurried to the front door. Zander was right behind her. "Come on. I'm late enough as it is."

He didn't say a word, just followed her.

In the car, Charlie ignored the heat of her blush, and bit her lip while Zander merged into traffic. She wasn't sure if he was happy about her confession or if it scared the shit out of him.

It scared her.

She didn't have a great history with men. Well, one man. Her experience might not be considered a history, really. She rubbed at the building tension in her shoulders. It seemed like seconds later, Zander parked the car a block away from the shop.

Cars, people, and police officers were on the street. She hadn't seen so much activity in this part of town before. Her smile was wide. "Wow, this is great."

"Sure is," Zander said. "It's because of you."

"No." She opened the car door. "It's because everyone spread the word and the Jordans are good people."

She met Zander at the front of the car and held his hand while they hurried through the crowd to the shop. She spotted Carl, a head taller than most.

He looked at her and smiled. "There you are. What happened?"

"Long story. How's it going? Is Rebecca here?"

"Yeah. She wants to see you. She has an apartment on the second floor. Go to the back of the storage room. Up the stairs." He pointed. "We're not letting many through that door. Decker is a little overwhelmed with everything."

"Okay." She tugged Zander through the crowd.

Her spirit rode high on the idea that Rebecca would be able to keep the store open. Charlie needed a mug that matched the one she had picked up the first day she flipped the coin. The coin flip that brought her here.

She ducked past the door, and the crowd noise dropped a few levels. The storage area had boxes piled against the outside walls and into a small island in the middle of the room. Bright lights helped her spot the stairs at the back. But when she started up, Zander tugged back. She lost her balance and slammed into him, front to front.

He hugged her, kissed her neck. "You can't land a important statement like that on me and then not talk about it."

"I don't know that I want to talk about it," she said. "I'm scared. My first relationship—"

He cut her words off with a kiss that curled her toes in her shoes. She moaned, hugged him back, and returned the passion. Her breath caught in her chest. Heat exploded from her belly to the rest of her body. She shifted the angle of the kiss to get a better taste of his mouth, sinfully hot. Her fingers enjoyed the cool, silk strands of his dark hair.

She wanted closer, but this wasn't the time.

She inched out of the kiss and smiled up at him. "Nice."

"I love you too." He said. The sincerity in his stare dug under her skin and nestled there. He guided her away from him. "I wanted you to know."

A happy thump resonated in her chest.

At the top of the stairs, Rebecca stood beside a man in a wheelchair. He had dark hair and a thin face. His shoulders were wider than the chair, but his body seemed weak. He looked at her in surprise. Rebecca smiled and held her arms wide. "There she is."

Charlie approached Rebecca for a welcoming hug.

"I don't believe this." Zander's voice was breathy. "No fucking way."

Charlie looked over her shoulder at Zander's open mouthed, wide-eyed, expression. She asked, "What is it?"

"Zander?" Rebecca's husband said. His voice a small whisper. "Are you real?"

"Decker?" Zander rushed to the other man and fell to his knees in front of the chair. His eyes pooled with tears. "How is this possible? I've been looking everywhere for you."

"Hey, little brother." Decker threw his arms around Zander's shoulders and hugged tightly. "I missed you too. I've been looking for years too."

The men cried. Their low voices mingled with giddiness and awe.

It seemed this was the third brother, Zander's middle brother. Charlie's heartbeat skipped at the sight of the men embracing. She smiled and cried with the others. She wiped the tears from her cheeks while standing arm in arm with Rebecca.

"This is Zander?" Rebecca left Charlie to hug Zander. "Decker told me all about you. It's a miracle to find you."

"Zander, this is my wife. She's the light of my life." Decker smiled up at the two hugging. He rubbed his palm down his face and inhaled. "What a day!"

Chapter 21

Charlie stepped off the bus in front of Evergreen Medical Center. She had flipped the coin when she woke. The sixteenth flip read: GIVE BLOOD. She wished she had her umbrella and glared at the clouds above.

She couldn't find it and didn't know where she had left it last. Wind kicked her hair back from her face and she nestled deeper into her soft collar.

Zander, Corbin and Decker wanted time together today. She didn't blame them. They had a lot to catch up on.

She told Rebecca she would stop by later to help restock the shelves from yesterday's grand reopening. First, she wanted to follow the coin. Everything seemed to work out so far and she had five more flips left.

Her steps were lighter, faster, and eager in crossing the street. She wanted the next adventure. She liked having a purpose, having an impact on the world.

A volunteer inside the semi-crowded hospital directed Charlie to the blood bank. Charlie sat, unable to stop smiling, and spoke with the nurse taking her blood.

The nurse's name was Bernice. The older woman had a great sense of humor and a kind smile. Charlie liked her soft voice. Bernice was telling a story about her son because Charlie had mentioned witnessing the birth yesterday.

She said, "He's so great with kids. It's a shame he can't find work. People don't like the idea of a male nanny, I guess."

"I've got some new friends who just had a baby. I'll keep you in mind if they're looking for help." Charlie didn't know anything about nannies or raising children. She and Zander were far from that big commitment. She could imagine having them with him, though. The more she thought about her relationship with him, the more she loved life.

Bernice removed the needle from Charlie's arm and held a cotton ball over the bead of blood. "Hold that for a second." She attached a strip of tape and wheeled away on her chair. "How are you feeling?"

"Better than ever."

"There are snacks and juice outside the door. Please help yourself before you leave. I've enjoyed your company. Thanks for being such a good listener."

Charlie nodded, slowly got up, and realized she was fine on her feet. She grabbed a juice box and a package of cookies on her way out of the hospital. After a few steps, she dug the coin out of her pocket and flipped.

End over end, the coin sparkled in the hallway. It landed in her palm and she read the inscription: GIVE A GIFT. 17/21.

She looked up and spotted Juan. "Hey."

"I was just getting some food." He gestured at the cafeteria signs.

Charlie smiled. "How's your boy?"

"He's healthy. Amy is healthy too." His smile took up most of his face.

"Well, congratulations." Charlie placed her hand on his arm and squeezed.

"Thanks for all the help. Couldn't have done it without you."

"It was my pleasure." She dropped her hand. "Hey, you might want to talk with Suzie and Milt about a new place to live. Those apartments on the fourth floor don't have tenants. I'll pay for your first three months."

"Really?" He ducked his head. "You're already paying the hospital bill."

"Consider the three months a gift. My congratulations gift for the new baby."

He nodded. A blush formed on his cheeks. "You're too nice."

"Thank you for letting me help, Juan. It makes me happy."

He nodded again and headed down the hall.

Charlie stepped out of the hospital and into the rain with her shoulders held high and a plan in her mind about Juan. She needed to talk with Milt about how it would all work. Certain the situation was under control, she fished out the coin from her pocket.

The coin's sparkle didn't disappoint even in the heavy, dark clouds and dim light today. Gold flashed, the coin rotated end over end, and she caught her breath. The coin landed in her palm. She loved the little zing up to her elbow, the warmth.

The new words read: INVITE A FRIEND TO DINNER. 18/21.

She closed her eyes and inhaled. "Who?"

She answered, "Beth."

She wanted to talk with her best friend and tonight was great timing. She texted encouragement to Zander and sent an email to Beth about meeting for dinner. The boys were busy and it was a great time to have a girls' night.

Charlie flipped the coin again. This time the words read: HAVE SOME TEA. 19/21.

Lance came into her thoughts. She nodded, tucked the coin into her pocket, and ran for the next bus. The uneventful ride had her looking at her phone, answering texts and sending thanks email to everyone for the successful reopening of Rebecca's store.

The bus stopped and she thanked the driver on her way out.

Rain soaked her shoulders. Her hair flattened against her head and dripped into her face. She stepped over a puddle and paused at the pothole she had found the coin in weeks ago. Carefully, she eased around the hole. There were a couple of cars parked out front. Nobody walked around the area.

Warmth inside the Green Leaf and Brew caused a shiver along her spine. She shook her jacket off and gasped. Her umbrella sat in a metal tube by the door. Her heart hammered in her chest at the coincidence. She remembered that it had been raining the night she had visited the shop.

"Charlie?" She looked up and across the empty shop at Lance. "Wow."

Charlie smiled, approached Lance at the bar, and ignored the strange smells in the shop as she passed the bookshelves. "How are you?"

He came around the bar. His sleeves were rolled up to his elbows. "I'm doing well. What about you?"

"I'm happy to see you're not in jail."

He laughed. "Can I make you a cup of coffee? The weather…" He shook his head.

"Tea?" She nodded, found a seat at the bar, and shrugged out of her coat.

"Have you seen Zander?" Lance asked while he fixed her drink.

"Yes. Have you?"

"No." He used a interesting machine then set the mug in front of her. He leaned on his elbows with a big smile. "It's a shame. I liked that guy even though he's a cop."

She didn't want to share her relationship with anyone right now, least of all a man Zander had arrested. Instead, she asked, "How's Lily?"

"Well." Lance exhaled. He speared his hands through his hair and shook his head. "The trial was tough. She'll be spending a lot of time in prison for what she did."

"I'm sorry to hear that." Charlie blew over the hot liquid in the cup.

"I'm not."

She lifted her eyebrows. "No?"

"She'll get the help she needs in prison. That's no life for anyone. I just wished she had listened to me in the first place."

Charlie picked up the tea and nodded. She spilled the liquid over her chest. A yelp came out of her mouth. Heat exploded on her cheeks due to embarrassment. Lance handed her a towel to clean up the splotch while they laughed.

From there, the visit was fun. Charlie smiled on the bus ride to Jordan's corner store. She entered the business and got right to work restocking the shelves. Rebecca introduced Charlie to a worker named LeeAnn before she excused herself for a nap.

Charlie finished the work, bought a mug with a smiley-face shot in the forehead, made a phone call, and hurried back to her apartment for dinner with Beth. She flipped the coin.

It said: GIVE A SINCERE HUG. 20/21.

Charlie met the pizza guy at the apartment gate and rushed to her place with the hot food. She set the pizza, a two-liter bottle of soda, and cheesy sticks on the table. In the kitchen, she fed Shadow. She shrugged out of her jacket, draped it over a chair at the table.

A knock came at the door before Beth stepped inside.

"Hey Charlie," Beth said with a hug. When they separated, Beth took off her wet jacket and draped it over a different chair. She set a book on the table. The title of the book read: *Change A Habit In 21 Days*.

Beth said, "I'm so hungry."

Charlie sat across from Beth. They ate in silence for a moment. Charlie reread the title to Beth's book and fished the coin out of her jacket pocket on the back of the chair. She turned it in her fingers in thought.

"How's the flipping going?" Beth poured more soda into her cup as Charlie studied the gold flecks in the metal. Charlie said, "I don't understand it. Things are different when I flip it now."

"I'll say," Beth cheered.

Charlie looked at her friend.

"You're a different person. You're no longer looking for things that are bad. You've embraced living happy." Beth shrugged. "Maybe that's what the coin was meant to do. Help you change your point of view."

Charlie did feel different, more thankful and giving. More fulfilled. The empty abyss in her chest twenty-one flips ago was gone. It was filled with good friends and a newfound purpose of helping people. Beth might have a point.

"I've got one more flip."

"Yeah?" She saw Beth shrug again. "I don't think you need it anymore."

Charlie nodded. She flipped the coin for the last time. It sparkled, flashed, and held her attention like always. This time, the metal was cool in her palm. She read the etched words out loud with a smile.

"LOSE THIS COIN."

Best wishes to all.

Be sure to check out my other books and thank you
for reading.
www.Judy@Judydawn.com

About The Author

Judy Dawn writes magical realism encouraging hope, love, and the pursuit of happiness. She integrates fantasy into real world environments with romantic elements. Her contemporary Men of Snow stories have thrilled e-readers since 2010 and Amazon placed *A Secret Gift* on the recommended reading list. Those who like uplifting endings will enjoy Judy Dawn's unconventional stories about the magic of love.